# ENDLESS KNIGHT

MIDNIGHT EMPIRE: THE RESTORATION, BOOK 1

ANNABEL CHASE

RED PALM PRESS LLC

Copyright © 2022 by Annabel Chase

All rights reserved.

No part of this book may be reproduced in any form or by any electronic or mechanical means, including information storage and retrieval systems, without written permission from the author, except for the use of brief quotations in a book review.

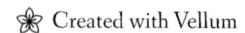

Created with Vellum

## PROLOGUE

Selma stared into the flames like a woman possessed. Her close-set eyes were unnaturally round and milky white. Instead of her usual hunched shoulders, the witch's body was rigid and straight. Talia was convinced that rigor mortis had somehow set in before death. She longed to test her theory. As Talia raised a finger to poke the older witch on the shoulder, a firm hand smacked hers away.

"Leave her be," Kathleen hissed.

Talia could always count on Kathleen to interfere, like that time Talia was finally going to succeed with a transmogrification spell and Kathleen swooped in like a vampire and stomped out the magic. Kathleen was only a middling witch, but she acted like she was as powerful as Selma and the other elders. Talia's parents had advised her to stop aggravating Kathleen. She would if she knew how. Kathleen seemed to relish their unpleasant encounters and Talia was convinced the middling witch went out of her way to keep tabs on the younger generation.

An ear-splitting scream sent Talia scrambling away

from the bonfire. Selma's head jerked back and black smoke poured from her mouth, reminding Talia of a chimney—if chimneys were made of flesh and bone and absolutely terrifying.

"Blood," Selma screeched. "Our misery and our salvation!"

Her body contorted again. The witch dropped to her hands and knees. The top of her head narrowly missed the flames. Kathleen rushed forward and helped the old witch to her feet.

"What did you see?" Kathleen prompted.

Talia hurried closer so as not to miss a single word. The older witches were always so secretive. Talia didn't understand the point of being part of a coven when they so often excluded people. The right age. The right magic. The right pedigree. The right allegiance. All were necessary in order to live in their Lancaster enclave. Talia knew her parents fell somewhere in the middle, which likely meant she did too. Talia didn't care about power, but she had a thirst for knowledge that went unquenched. The coven controlled the flow of information and the drips that fell to Talia were deeply unsatisfying. Maybe someday when she was older, she would leave this place and be sated.

Selma's eyes returned to their normal brown. "We must send a message. Hurry, fetch the birds!"

Kathleen leaned forward and whispered, "Are the birds a wise choice? A horde of butterflies was spotted fifteen miles northeast of here not three hours ago."

"They are safer than sending a messenger on foot."

*And more disposable*, Talia thought, although she was fond of the birds they kept in the aviary. To the untrained eye, the birds lived freely in the forest. That part of the forest was warded with magic to keep the trees alive, which was legal, and also to prevent the birds from leaving of their own accord. The latter was an illegal use of magic and Talia knew the coven would be in grave danger if it was ever discovered. Vampires didn't allow the use of magic except under certain circumstances and sending secret messages behind their backs wasn't one of them.

Kathleen snapped her fingers. "Scribe, where are you?"

Another witch rushed forward. Helen. She was dutiful and organized and had the neatest handwriting Talia had ever seen. The perfect scribe for the coven.

Selma described what she'd seen in her vision and repeated the words she'd shrieked, although Talia doubted it was necessary to repeat them. Everybody in Lancaster County had likely heard the screams about blood.

"Does your vision make sense in the context of the others?" Helen asked.

Selma nodded.

Talia followed the trio of witches to the aviary. The older witches were too engrossed in conversation to notice. Talia watched as two cardinals were sent with two identical messages. They were female cardinals, which meant their colors were more muted. Talia had once asked why they didn't send the red cardinals. Selma explained that it was better to blend in because it increased your chances of survival. Red drew the eye, particularly the eye of a vampire, and was best avoided. In fact, anything that attracted vampires was best avoided. Selma even confessed that she'd once sanctioned the expulsion of a child because her magic endangered them all.

"What type of magic could endanger a coven?" Talia had wondered aloud.

Selma hadn't answered, but Talia could tell from the older witch's hard expression that she had no regrets about the decision.

Talia stood at the entrance to the aviary and watched the birds fly away. She said a little prayer to the gods for them, even though prayers were discouraged by the coven. There was no higher power, they told her. If there were, the Great Eruption wouldn't have occurred all those years ago and monsters would've stayed in the deep recesses of the earth where they belonged. There'd be no Eternal Night and the sun's rays would still reach the earth. Vampires wouldn't have been able to seize control of the world and outlaw magic.

So Talia kept her prayers to herself.

The witches kept their eyes turned skyward, as though they could see beyond the blanket of darkness that smothered them each and every day. They were too engrossed in their actions to notice Talia.

"You're certain it's her?" Kathleen asked.

"Prophecies are never certain. You know that," Selma said.

"You remember what happened at the market. That was years ago. There's no telling what she's capable of now."

Selma leveled her companion with a look. "There are greater threats to our survival."

"She's a different kind of threat," Kathleen insisted.

Selma remained resolute. "Which is why she is needed. The outcome might enable us to see the bigger picture."

"There is so much at stake..." Helen interjected.

The women started to walk away and Talia strained to hear them.

"If she fails now," Selma said, "it is no loss to us and our hands remain clean."

"And if she fails later?" Kathleen pressed.

Talia released a soft gasp when she heard the words that followed.

"Then may the gods help us all."

# ONE

I sat on a ledge with my legs dangling over the side of a red brick building. If I didn't have a job to do, I'd take time to enjoy the quiet of the neighborhood. Hudson Square was one of the least populated areas in the city, which meant fewer lights and less foot traffic. It wasn't always like this. According to royal records, it was once a hub for large media companies. The blocks heaved with luxury high-rise buildings and glass monuments to technology. When the neighborhood's fortunes rose, it became a sought-after location close to the Hudson River.

When the neighborhood's fortunes fell, they fell hard.

The simultaneous eruption of ten of the world's supervolcanoes resulted in enough ash in the atmosphere to block the sun. The Eternal Night wasn't the only outcome.

When darkness fell, the monsters came.

Deep in the earth's core, they bided their time until ten doors opened and allowed them entry. By land, sea, and air they attacked and invaded. Active calderas in the Americas and Australasia meant those areas suffered more than other continents. The entire continent of South America succumbed to the magma and monsters. Here in Hudson Square, they managed to wipe out most of the skyscrapers and destroy half the neighborhood before the vampires were able to secure it. Its proximity to the Hudson River became a negative feature. The damage was psychological as well as physical. Residents circumvented this neighborhood even after all these years, which was the reason House August refused to invest in its restoration. A shame, really. The place had potential.

I leaned over the ledge. There were five stories between my feet and the pavement. Thankfully I didn't mind heights. Sometimes I fantasized that a mighty dragon would breach the city wards and whisk me away. When I was feeling particularly lonely, the dragon would turn out to be a hot dragon shifter who fell madly in love with me. Too bad dragon shifters didn't exist.

I kept my eye on the defunct Big Apple tour bus parked on the street below. My boss hated when anybody referred to the city as 'the Big Apple,' which only encouraged me to do it as frequently as possible. As the Director of Security for House August, Olis had a lot of responsibility and the wizard didn't suffer fools gladly.

In other words, he was a joy to torment.

Bored, I scraped the dirty heels of my boots against the brick. I would've preferred to drop down and confront the occupants of the bus right now. Get the confrontation over with. I knew I couldn't do that, though. My recklessness was the reason I was here in the first place, working for House August as an indentured servant in their security division. Thanks to my actions, I'd been given a choice—a public beheading in Times Square or servitude. I chose the latter. I wasn't big on spectacles unless I was the one in charge of it. Now the royal vampires owned me. I was their tool. Arguably a tool was better than a weapon, which had been my life before this one. 'Death Bringer' they called me, among other things. The moniker was a little on the nose for my taste, but it conveyed the right message. I was both feared and revered by vampires because of my rare type of magic.

I rubbed an apple on my chest and bit into it. One of the perks of my position was decent food. No need to scavenge or starve. House August owned magical orchards and vineyards on Long Island. Unlike me, those witches and wizards were compensated for their work. If I'd been a regular witch, maybe they would've offered me a cushy job like that—help them grow their blueberries and blackberries or tend to the grapes that made the wine.

Sadly I wasn't that kind of witch. My magic had limited uses, most of which involved death.

I watched with interest as a rat emerged from a nearby dumpster and scrambled toward the bus. Rats had been a real problem in the city in the early years of the Eternal Night. They'd once been as small as cats, but the changing environment created fertile ground for their evolution. When House August seized control of the city, one of their first acts was to deal with the growing rat population. It wasn't as altruistic as it sounded. The rats were spreading disease among the human population and the vampires needed human blood to survive, which made rats Public Enemy Number One.

The rat headed straight for the bus and I suspected it sensed food inside. From my vantage point, I could see the dumpster was empty. I gave House August credit—the royal family was serious about sanitation.

The rat scampered toward the bus and stopped short about a foot from the bus's exterior. I watched carefully.

"Come on, buddy. Don't give up yet. One more try," I said under my breath.

The rat started forward but only made it an inch before it bounced backward.

"And that's a wrap, folks," I said to no one in particular.

I finished the apple and threw the core to the back of the alley. I had a good arm. The security team even tried to recruit me for the House softball team, but Olis refused permission. Only employees were allowed to play under the stadium lights, not indentured servants. Their loss.

The rat turned and lumbered toward its snack.

In the distance I spotted movement. A rabble of butterflies meant vampire patrol. I recognized the orange and black colors of Doug's team and checked my watch. Yep. Right on schedule.

Most people broke into an anxiety rash when they noticed a cluster of butterflies headed in their direction. Not me. I knew most of the vampires in the city, at least the ones with the ability to transform into butterflies. House August was smart enough to employ any vampire with advanced abilities, which was probably one of the reasons the royal family had managed to amass so much power. And even if I didn't recognize a particular vampire, there was a decent chance they'd recognize me.

The bus rocked once from side to side. Blue light flashed around it.

Time to go.

I retrieved a pocket knife from my utility belt and waited for the air to grow still. No sense letting a breeze thwart my plan. I sliced my palm and let three drops of blood fall to the pavement just outside the bus.

That ought to do the trick.

I watched the tiny sparks with satisfaction. They

must've decided the ancient bus was a decent hiding spot and they didn't need a stronger ward.

They'd be wrong.

I hooked a bungee cord to the ledge and shimmied down the side of the building. The lack of light in this neighborhood would make my entrance easier.

When I reached the second floor, I released the cord and jumped. My boots hit the top of the bus with a thud. Not quite the nimble landing I intended. From there I jumped to the pavement.

The door jerked open and a head popped out to investigate the sound. I grabbed him by the neck and slammed him against the side of the bus, squeezing hard. "I could've sworn I heard somebody speaking Latin in there. Know anything about that?"

He struggled to speak but no words came out. No surprise since I was pressing on his windpipe.

"Inquisitor," somebody yelled from inside the bus.

"Tell your buddies I'm not an inquisitor." I noticed the man's bulging eyes. "Hold on. I can see you're busy. I'll tell them." Still gripping his neck, I poked my head inside the open door. "Hey, guys. Just FYI, I'm not an inquisitor."

Another man ran to the door. Visible blue veins and a bright red scar made his face look like a topographical map featuring a river of blood.

Scarface shook a fist at me. "May the sun make you perish!"

"Ooh, burn. The ultimate insult. If I were a vampire, I'd be deeply offended."

"You're a disgrace to your kind."

"Takes one to know one." Very mature, I realized, but it was the first comeback that came to mind. "What are you guys doing in there? I saw blue light so unless you're having a special sale..."

Fingers dug into my hand and I released my grip on the man's neck. I wasn't trying to kill him, although I was sure he didn't see it that way.

I grabbed him by the collar and dragged him inside the bus. There were four men total and evidence of magic everywhere. Wizards. A redhead attempted to clear the contraband from view.

"Don't bother, Clifford. I've already seen it."

The redhead frowned. "Clifford?"

"The Big Red Dog?" I made a noise of exasperation. "Did no one here read children's books? No wonder you turned to a life of crime."

"If you're not an inquisitor, then why do you care if we use magic?" my former chokehold victim asked.

"I work for House August and your little activities here are considered a security threat."

"You're one of us. How can you work for them?" Clifford asked.

"First, I'm not one of you. Second, we all do what we have to do to survive."

"If that's what you believe, then you should let us go," the curly-haired wizard said. "We're only trying to do the same." He wore wire-rimmed spectacles and a T-shirt bearing an image of the Statue of Liberty. Instead of a torch, she held a wand.

"No, you're trying to use magic for your own selfish purposes, which is illegal."

"It isn't selfish to want to feed our families," Clifford said. "This is the only avenue available to us."

"You're lucky I'm the one finding you. Anybody else

would've dragged the four of you into Times Square for a beheading and made a public spectacle of your deaths."

The curly-haired wizard eyed me carefully. "You're not going to do that?"

"No."

"Why not?" Scarface asked.

"Because I'm in a good mood and I've decided to let you off with a warning."

"You have the authority to do that?" the redhead asked.

I tapped my chin. "Let me think. Are you going to tell anyone?"

Clifford shook his head. "Not me. Why are you in a good mood?"

"Aw, I'm so glad you asked. You see, I have it on good authority that the taco truck on Eighth Avenue is getting a shipment of avocados this week. Do you know what that means?"

They shook their heads.

I clapped my hands. "Guacamole, people. Come on."

It was the little things that made life worth living. It had been at least a year since my last taste of guacamole and that was only because I'd worked security for the king and queen's anniversary party at the royal compound and snuck as many guacamole-laden nibbles as I could manage without getting caught.

"I'm allergic to avocado," Clifford said.

I rolled my eyes. "Of course you are."

"Why were you watching us if you didn't know what we were doing?" Scarface asked.

"I was made aware of an illegal shipment of mint to Battery Park and traced one of the larger deliveries to this bus."

Scarface elbowed Clifford in the gut. "I told you not to purchase so much of it at once. Small transactions only."

"I've been waiting for a couple days for something to happen and finally it did." I clapped my hands once in dramatic fashion. "Let there be blue light!"

"We're not hurting anybody," Scarface complained.

"You're hurting the system. Magic is against the law unless you have special dispensation like me. Latin is forbidden. Mint is for vampires only. End of story."

"Vampires only outlawed magic because they know that witches and wizards would be able to overthrow them with it," Clifford said.

Arms crossed, I looked down my nose at him. "And what magic spell would be powerful enough to eradicate vampire rule? I'd love to know."

I turned to look at the fourth wizard who'd been silent this whole time and it was then that I saw it.

The makings of a magical bomb.

My stomach lurched. These wizards weren't simply buying mint for healing tonics or their tea. I'd bet good money they were the wizards responsible for the subway bombing last month. Witnesses described a flash of blue light before the station blew up.

My gaze shifted from the bomb to Scarface. Our eyes locked and I saw the glimmer of recognition in his eyes.

"Displodo!" he yelled.

A snapping sound followed.

The four wizards shot out of the bus like their clothes were on fire. It took me a second but I got there in the end. A magical bomb was about to explode two feet away from me.

Terrific.

Blue light flashed in waves and I felt my body fly sideways and slam against a hard surface. Metal creaked and groaned. I toppled outside and landed on the pavement flat on my stomach. The inside of my mouth tasted like blood and my one eye didn't seem to want to open. Pain bloomed on the side of my head.

Those slimy bastards. I should've rounded them up and presented them to Olis on a platter. Freakin' Clifford. I bet the only thing big about him was his cowardice.

I gave myself a minute to recover from the blast. The bus was in pieces around me. No doubt all evidence of magic was gone. I'd have to track the four wizards from scratch.

I heard the crunch of metal as someone slowly and methodically made their way toward me. A Good Samaritan, mayhap? Unlikely. We didn't have many of those in the city. It was everyone for themselves. Only vampires could afford to be magnanimous, not that it was in their nature. In my experience, they were inherently selfish creatures.

I lifted my chin off the ground and looked directly at a pair of familiar black boots. They were distinctive in that they bore the triquetra on each tongue. I only knew this because I'd been forced to scrub them on multiple occasions after incidents that may or may not have been my fault.

I turned my head sideways and peered up at my boss. "Hey, Olis."

The wizard regarded me from beneath a line of judgmental peach fuzz that masqueraded as eyebrows. "Back to your usual shenanigans, I see."

I scrambled to my feet. "Mission accomplished, sir."

He waved a hand. "You call this mess an accomplishment?"

"I know what the mint is being used for. That's the important part. Who cares about a teeny tiny explosion?"

"I believe it was Machiavelli who said that the ends justify the means," Olis replied. "Is that the kind of person you'd like to align yourself with?"

"I work for vampires, sir." I shot an apologetic look at the vampire beside him. "No offense, Bruno."

Bruno shrugged. He was the most lackadaisical vampire I'd ever met, which was probably the reason he ended up on a security team alongside a witch and a wizard.

"Anyway, Machiavelli is widely misunderstood," I continued.

Olis observed me with a mixture of amusement and irritation. "How so?"

"The concept is more complex. It doesn't mean we can do what we want without consequences as long as the outcome is favorable."

"Then what does it mean?" Olis asked.

I sighed. "Read *The Prince* and then *Discourses on Livy* and you'll get a fuller picture."

"How do you know all that?" Bruno asked.

"Because I communicate with his ghost at night."

For a split second, Bruno looked like he might believe me. Then his raised brow morphed into a scowl.

"From books." I patted his chest. "You should visit the library sometime. You might learn why you can't transform into a butterfly like your superior vampire buddies."

Bruno's fangs snapped into place and I laughed.

Olis stepped between us. "Is that wise, Bruno?"

The vampire's nostrils flared. "I'm not afraid of you, Britt the Bloody."

I pointed at him. "That attitude right there proves how desperately you need an education."

Olis grabbed me by the elbow and steered me away

before things escalated. "Bruno, pick through the debris and see what you can find," he called over his shoulder.

Good. Let Bruno do the grunt work for a change.

"Do you want me to write up a report on what I found? I think it's connected to the subway bombing last month."

Olis blinked rapidly. "Later. There's a more pressing matter."

I frowned. "More pressing than a magical bomb?"

"Your presence has been requested. That's the reason I'm here."

"Really? I thought you were here to discipline me."

"For what?"

"Nothing," I said quickly. He didn't need to know that I'd intended to let the four escaped wizards go—before I discovered their treachery, of course.

"The queen has asked for you personally."

I looked at him askance. "Queen Dionne?"

"Is there any other?"

"Well, let me think. There's Queen Margot and Queen Iris. Is there a Queen Britannia or did I make that one up?"

He sighed in exasperation. "Is there any other queen who would summon you?"

"Technically, no, although I don't know why Queen Dionne would want to see me. I don't think she knows my name."

I rarely interacted with the queen. With King Maxwell on a business trip and the prince-who-shall-not-be-named holding down the fort in the Southern Territories, Queen Dionne must've had no choice but to summon me herself.

"Clearly she knows it well enough to send for you. Does everything have to be combative with you?"

"The last time I exchanged words with the queen, it was for the king to offer me the choice between death and a life of servitude. Forgive me if I'm not in a hurry to relive that moment."

Olis loosened his grip on my elbow. "I'm sure whatever the queen has in store for you—it isn't death."

Fear gathered at the base of my tongue and I swallowed. "I've never known you to be wrong, Olis. Do me a favor and don't start now."

# TWO

The wizard guided me to the corner of Spring Street and Sixth Avenue.

I laughed. "We're not seriously taking the subway."

There were only a few active subways left in the city. After the Great Eruption, the underground system became a hodgepodge of monster lairs and human hideouts. I'd been down there many times, but it was never my first choice.

Olis descended the steps without a response.

I quickly followed behind him. "This is a strange way to reach the compound. Even with your bony old-man legs, walking uptown is faster."

The House August compound was located at 212 Fifth Avenue with views of downtown and Madison Square Park. Once a luxury condominium complex, the royal vampire family claimed the entire building as their own. Staff members and servants lived in the buildings immediately surrounding it. In vampire circles, living close to the compound was a sign of social status, which meant real estate prices in this neck of the woods were sky high.

Olis's voice echoed below ground. "Be grateful it's the subway. It could be worse."

"New Jersey?"

Olis kept his gaze straight ahead as we plunged into total darkness. "You joke, but there was an unfortunate incident there last week."

"Only last week?"

"Two warring werewolf packs annihilated each other in Vineland. They ravaged each other until there was basically nothing left. By the time our security team arrived, only their bones remained."

I cringed. "Thanks for the visual. Is that why you're bringing me down here—to discuss the intricacies of pack politics? Because I can think of more charming places to have that discussion."

He stopped walking for a moment to regard me. "What have I told you about asking so many questions?"

"That you wish you had my inquisitive mind?"

The wizard held up a wand tipped in light and guided me to a tunnel. "In here."

The hairs on the back of my neck stood at attention. "Olis, what's going on? If you want to get rid of me, there are easier ways."

Lights flashed and I noticed a disused subway carriage on the tracks. The metal was bent and rusted on the side facing me. The doors opened and Olis nudged me forward. I stumbled into the carriage and the doors creaked shut behind me.

Queen Dionne sat alone in a row of orange seats. If I hadn't known I was meeting her, I wouldn't have recognized her. Her dark curls were hidden beneath a wool cap and she wore a black turtleneck beneath a grey coat. The queen was regaled as a fashion icon—she was the beauty to her husband's beast—but no one would be admiring her in this ensemble. They'd have to notice her first.

I bowed. "Your Majesty."

"Sit, Britta."

I debated correcting her but decided to leave it alone. If the queen decided I was Britta instead of Britt, the additional 'a' wasn't the hill I wanted to die on.

I sat in the row of orange seats directly across from her on the opposite side of the carriage. I made a concerted effort not to slouch. I sat with my back straight and both feet flat on the floor. Olis would be proud. Apparently my posture was often 'lacking,' along with my manners. I blamed my wild upbringing.

I met the queen's gaze and noticed her red-rimmed eyes. This wasn't the work of the queen's makeup artist.

"How may I be of service, Your Majesty?" There were questions I'd rather ask, but this seemed like the most appropriate one.

She cut to the chase. "There's been an incident and I need a trusted member of our security team to travel to the Southern Territories. I've decided you, Britta, are that trusted member."

"Why me?"

"Olis is needed here. He recommended you. Says you're the most capable and that's what I need for this task."

I stifled a laugh. The last time Olis complimented me, it was because I managed to hoodwink Bruno into giving me the coveted dinner party shift. If there was spare food to be found, I made sure I was well-positioned to claim it.

"Well, I'll have to thank him when I leave here. Maybe send a gift basket."

The queen didn't seem bothered by my insolence.

"And what do I do when I get to the Southern Territories?"

"Find my son in Palm Beach and escort him home."

I strangled a cough. "Your son?"

"Prince Alaric."

I knew his name. I just refused to say it. "You want me to travel all the way to Palm Beach and bring His Royal Highness back to New York?" The words nearly got stuck in my throat and I had to force them out.

She clasped her hands in her lap. "That's right."

"I'm sorry, Your Majesty. I don't think that's such a good idea."

Her head snapped to attention. "I beg your pardon?"

*Tread carefully*, I warned myself. "I'm not sure I'm the right one for the job." I couldn't offer the real reason.

"Nonsense. Olis says you're the best there is and I only want the best for my son. The future of House August depends on it."

"What kind of security threat are we looking at?" I was already calculating which weapons to pack. Although my best weapon was the magic that flowed through my veins, it wasn't always the best option.

The queen averted her gaze. "I wish I knew."

"Has someone made threats against the prince's life?" Even the word 'prince' tasted like acid on my tongue.

"Indirectly." She drew a shaky breath and returned her focus to me. "This information goes no further. You must swear an oath. The only ears this news reaches belong to my son."

I clutched my fist over my heart and bowed. "I'll tell no one, Your Majesty. You have my word."

"The king is dead."

We stared at each other for what seemed like an eternity. However long it actually was gave me ample time to memorize each gold fleck in her hazel eyes. My stomach churned. Those gold flecks haunted my dreams.

I finally found my voice. "How? When?"

"Last night. The messenger reached me this morning. Their party was ambushed outside Pittsburgh."

"Wasn't he on a business trip?" I recalled Olis mentioning something about a visit to a factory in connection with the manufacture of synthetic blood. The idea was catching fire overseas and House August was eager to jump on the bandwagon and meet demand. King Maxwell wanted to be the first on this continent to embrace the trend and shift away from a dependence on natural blood. It wasn't unusual for the king to attend to matters in person. His desire for control extended to even the most menial tasks.

"Yes. His itinerary was public knowledge. A regrettable mistake. At this point we only know that he was murdered. Nothing more."

I frowned. "What about the messenger? Couldn't they say what happened?"

"He succumbed to his wounds as he delivered the news. Poison."

I slumped against the seat. King Maxwell was dead. The most powerful vampire in North America, ruler of House August, had been assassinated.

"Has anyone claimed responsibility for the attack?"

She shook her head. "And as long as no one does, we have room to maneuver. I need this kept quiet. The entire realm is at risk if word gets out too soon."

"Which is why you need me to escort the prince home."

"Exactly."

"Why not send troops to retrieve him?"

"Because I don't want to attract attention to him. I want you to stay off the main roads. You were once a traveler. You must know how to stick to the shadows."

Traveler was the polite way of saying assassin.

"I do."

"I have no idea which group murdered my husband, but it stands to reason they will be after Alaric next. Wipe out father and son and they've eliminated any hope of succession."

"And you're not sending anyone else. Only me?" Although I was no stranger to dangerous jobs, it seemed ironic that the job to protect someone would be the most dangerous one of all.

Queen Dionne observed me. Her solemn and grief-stricken eyes were now shrewd and calculating. "I understand how treacherous a journey this might be. That's why I'm willing to make you an offer you can't refuse."

"I didn't realize I had the option to refuse being an indentured servant and all."

The queen scrutinized me. "You and I both know what you can do. You could kill me right now and no one would be able to stop you in time."

"Maybe not, but they'd kill me soon enough afterward. I have no interest in regicide, Your Majesty." I also had no interest in hiding for the rest of my life. If I killed the queen, I could kiss creature comforts goodbye for good. I'd end up living in a cave in South America where no one from House August could hunt me down.

"I'm glad to hear it."

My curiosity was officially piqued. "What kind of offer?"

She pressed her palms flat on the seat on either side of her. "Your freedom."

My pulse sped up. "My freedom? You can do that?"

"I'm the queen. Of course I can. Return my son safely to the compound and I'll release you from your servitude. You have my word."

It really was an offer I couldn't refuse. I'd gladly suck up the close proximity to the devil in exchange for my freedom.

"I'll leave tomorrow."

"I've already made the arrangements for your transport. You'll leave tonight."

"Will it be safe?"

She wore a sad smile. "Is anything in this world safe?"

"No, Your Majesty."

"I don't see why anyone would follow you, if that's what you're asking. The only one who knows of our arrangement is Olis. One of the reasons I asked you to meet me here is so that no one would see you." She retrieved a small object from the folds of her dress, as well as a wad of cash. "Take these. You'll need that to persuade my son to listen."

"Yes, Your Majesty." Without looking, I tucked the object in my pocket.

"Good luck, Britta. Our future is in your hands."

My head spinning, I left the subway station and went straight home to pack. All I had to do was deliver the precious prince to his mother and freedom was mine. No more security sweeps. No more Bruno.

Sighing deeply, I surveyed my one-bedroom apartment. No more comfortable home. The apartment was typical for a member of the royal staff, although it was impressively nice compared to that of the general population. I'd have to find another place to live. There'd be cheaper places outside New York. If the prince was returning home for good, it made sense to put as much distance between us as possible.

I grabbed a bag and threw in a change of clothes, leaving

space for the most important items—weapons. Unlike most witches, I wasn't much of a cook so I used the oven as a small armory. I opened the oven door and withdrew two daggers, a handgun, and ammo. The snub-nosed Monster Masher was a relative of the Ruger LCR that humans once favored. A Ruger worked fine in a world dominated by humans. Not so much one crawling with monsters and supernaturals. Thus the Monster Masher was born.

I cringed at the sound of breaking glass in the bedroom. Leaving the weapons on the floor, I went to inspect the damage. A drinking glass was on the floor in pieces and a pygmy dragon perched on my bedside table with an incredibly guilty expression on his face. His rose-colored talons curved over the edge and I noticed fresh scrapes in the wood.

"George, what did you do?"

The miniature dragon turned his amber eye to me and burped. Puffs of smoke emanated from his little jaws.

I looked at the liquid that had spilled on the floor and remembered last night. George must've mistaken my leftover tequila for water. Typical George.

"What have I told you about touching my drinks? That tequila was a gift." A gift that I gave myself after swiping it from a royal party. No way could I afford tequila on my nonexistent salary.

George made a disgruntled sniffing sound and flew across the room to perch on top of the dresser while I cleaned up the mess.

"I need to take a trip for work," I told him as I emptied the glass fragments into the trashcan. "It should be a week, maybe more, depending on how much trouble we encounter."

At the mention of "we," George made a squawking

sound that reminded me of a parrot. It wasn't the only resemblance between them. Although his body was covered in yellow-gold scales, his wings were streaked with red and orange that gave the dragon a slightly tropical appearance.

I turned to look at him. "Not 'we' as in you and me. 'We' as in...someone else." I couldn't bring myself to say his name. George wasn't a fan of the vampire prince. The dragon had witnessed the relationship from beautiful beginning to bitter end and had made his feelings known.

George made a noise of protest.

I returned to packing, tossing in my phone and charger, and ignored his pleading looks. "This job is too dangerous for you and it involves travel."

Every time I placed an article of clothing in the bag, George swooped in and removed it. Finally I jerked the bag closed, and confronted him.

"I have to go find the prince, okay? He needs an escort back to New York. Queen's orders."

George expressed his displeasure by blowing smoke out of his nostrils.

"Please don't do that or you'll set off the fire alarm. Trust me. Nobody's less thrilled than I am." I resumed packing.

George flew out of the room to sulk. He wasn't a baby dragon, he just acted like one.

I'd encountered him on a job outside Atlanta. His wing was injured and he was missing an eye. I still didn't know what happened to cause his injuries. He looked so pathetic trying to fly to the top of the dumpster for scraps. With only one good wing, he kept sliding down to the ground. I didn't know what compelled me to step in. My friend Liam blamed secondhand embarrassment—that I couldn't bear to watch someone fail so completely—but he was wrong. I looked at that tiny, misfit dragon and saw myself fighting for survival with whatever tools I possessed. He looked pathetic, yes, but also determined. When I intervened, he was sliding down the side of the hulking metal container after another failed attempt. I fed him, mended his wing—there was nothing I could do for the eye—and we'd been together ever since.

It took me six months to give him a name. I kept expecting him to leave. Finally I grew tired of calling him generic names like "hey, you" and "baby dragon" and settled on George, after Curious George. As a kid in search of a home, I spent time with a human couple that owned a small library of children's books from when their own kids were young. The couple told me the story of the Jewish husband and wife fleeing Paris on bicycles in 1940 with the manuscript of the first book. Curious George quickly became my favorite. I loved the monkey's friendship with the Man in the Yellow Hat and that the Man looked out for George. It seemed like fate that George and I also ended up having adventures in New York City.

I eventually discovered that George disliked when I called him a baby dragon because he wasn't a baby at all. At the time, I didn't realize he was fully grown. I'd never heard of a pygmy dragon and assumed he was an abandoned infant. When he failed to grow, I assumed his growth had been stunted by his traumatic past. It was Olis who informed me that George was likely a pygmy and would never get any bigger. It eased my anxiety somewhat because I'd worried about where he would go when he outgrew my apartment. Dragons didn't live in New York City. There was a no-dragon policy in place and the city was warded to keep wild dragons at bay. House August employed a team of witches and wizards that made sure of it. Thankfully no one that noticed George objected to his presence—so far. Everyone found him too adorable to feel threatened by him. That was because they'd never accidentally stepped on his wing in a drunken stupor and lost all their leg hair in the process. I mean, arguably it was a win for me but it still hurt like the devil.

I zipped the bag and slung the strap over one shoulder. Then I retrieved my weapons from the floor of the kitchen, securing the daggers to the utility belt and the revolver in the holster. I added a black vest over my inventory. If there was one thing I did well it was hide. My weapons. My magic. Myself. I wouldn't have made it thirty years without that ability. It was a matter of self-preservation.

As I locked the apartment door, Liam Garrity appeared in the hallway. The werewolf worked as a civil engineer for House August and was the first and only neighbor to greet me when I moved in. Granted, he was blind drunk and carting around a backpack filled with explosives that would've taken down the whole building, but it was a nice gesture all the same.

He observed the bag on my shoulder. "Overnights with a new boyfriend already?"

"No. Just another job." I adored Liam, but the werewolf was notoriously nosy. If I said too much, he'd realize I was hiding something. Best to keep the conversation brief.

"Too bad. I'd like to see you dating again." Liam knew all about Prince Prick and hated the vampire, not that the prince even knew who Liam was. Like me, the werewolf was just another cog in the House August wheel.

"A love connection isn't my priority."

"Maybe it should be. You're wasting your youth. Why don't I ask around at the office? Plenty of hot, sweaty werewolves to choose from."

"No thanks." Liam had a habit of taking an average situation and making it exponentially worse. Sometimes there were incendiary devices involved. "Anyway, it isn't like I have free time to meet someone. That's how servitude works."

"Where's George?"

"Inside sulking because he can't come with me."

Liam frowned. "Why not?"

Damn. I really needed to stop talking. "Because it's indoors and he'll make a nuisance of himself. You know how he is."

"Dinner later?" he asked. "I have spaghetti. I'll need someone to chew the opposite end and meet me in the middle."

I smiled. "Try that cute guy in 5-D. I don't think I'll be back. It's a stakeout so it might last a few days. Don't worry if you don't see me around."

Liam gave me a funny look. "What's going on?"

I started toward the stairwell. "Nothing. Just running behind schedule. See you later."

I hurried down the steps before he could ask any follow-up questions. I hated lying to my friend, but it was far better than getting him killed for knowing too much.

# THREE

I handed my ticket to the collector and waited on the platform at August Station, formerly known as Penn Station. Most trains ran overground and even those weren't plentiful. The combination of supply chain issues and border disputes made train travel an undesirable option. Basically all means of transport were undesirable these days, which is why most of the population stayed put.

I boarded the train called the Silver Meteor that connected the city to Miami. The railroad line had fallen into disuse after the Great Eruption. Parts of the line had been destroyed by natural elements. Other parts by monsters. To their credit, House August restored the line and even added new tracks to allow the trains to circumvent the Wasteland once known as Washington D.C. that was inhabited by monsters. Some would argue that had always been the case. Now the train looped around the former nation's capital and connected Baltimore to Richmond. They had an ulterior motive, of course. The royal vampire family wanted a compound in Palm Beach and an easy way to travel between their two main residences. Once upon a time the entire family would decamp to Palm Beach for a few months each year and would commandeer the entire train to make room for their staff and personal belongings. That ended with the death of the elder prince, Theo. Rumor has it the grief-stricken queen refused to leave New York after the death of her son, as though Theo were lost instead of dead and might one day appear on her doorstep.

The doors opened and I found a seat near both an exit and a restroom. It was too long of a journey to trust my bladder. As the whistle blew and the doors began to close, George swooped into the carriage and settled on the seat beside me. I should've known he'd find a way to follow me. He was nothing if not resourceful.

I gave the pygmy dragon a pointed look. "What did you break?"

George's amber eye met mine.

I heaved a sigh. "You're lucky you're cute. If you ask me, it's your main survival skill."

I settled against the seat and leaned my head against the window. At some point, George fell asleep beside me. I only knew because he snored like an ogre after downing a keg of beer. Hopefully no one would complain about the noise. The carriage was mostly empty so the risk was low.

George's snoring aside, travel to Palm Beach was straightforward and uneventful as expected. I would've taken a boat if I had a death wish. There was no good water route anywhere. The ocean was teeming with monsters waiting for desperate or foolish sailors to happen by.

No one was looking for me, tracking me, or otherwise gave a rat's ass where I was headed. There were no checkpoints. I was traveling within House August territory, so I didn't need a travel pass or a form of ID. The only thing I needed was a way to get to the prince without being seen. Little did the queen know I had experience with exactly that.

I fell asleep somewhere around Savannah and woke up as we arrived at the station.

"Perfect timing," I said, stifling a yawn. I poked George awake and together we disembarked.

It felt good to stretch my legs so I opted to walk to my first destination, which wasn't the royal estate. If we wanted to lay low, the prince and I would need our own transportation to New York.

Cars weren't as prevalent now as they were when humans were in charge. Fuel was expensive and roads were long and dangerous. You never knew when you might encounter a roving pack of centaurs or a random demon. In my experience there was always the option of finding a very used car within striking distance of public transportation. Someone was always willing to pay for a set of wheels to complete their journey.

Today that someone was me.

The streets were relatively well-lit around the station which made it easier to find my way. If I needed an extra bit of light, George could burp a few flames. The dragon had his uses.

I found what I was looking for within two miles of the station—a small selection of used vehicles hawked by a guy named Skinny Pete. The name wasn't ironic. If Pete ate an apple, I was pretty sure I'd see the slight bulge in his stomach as he digested it.

I used some of the queen's cash for a green minivan that looked like it had been carting soccer moms and their kids since pre-Eternal Night days.

"Like new," Skinny Pete declared, beaming.

"Like hell," I replied.

But I took the keys anyway.

The royal residence was a far cry from the compound in New York. The sprawling estate was more of an adult playground than the massive building in the city. Security was far more lax here. I could've scaled the wall, climbed through the prince's window and killed him before anybody knew I'd set foot on the property. The prince was a powerful vampire, but he was more interested in using that power to spend money and get laid. With his father dead and his mother more of a figurehead, I wasn't sure what would become of House August. The prince I knew had no interest in being a leader. Then again, it had been three years since I'd last seen him.

Maybe he'd changed.

Loud music emanated from the yard and I realized I'd arrived in the midst of a party.

Okay, maybe he hadn't changed.

The gates opened to admit a stream of guests that had been waiting outside for admittance. I left the bag in the minivan and directed George to stay hidden there. I didn't trust the dragon not to cause a scene. He had a way of getting into mischief and now wasn't the time to clean up another one of his messes.

Lanterns lined the walkway that led to the backyard. The music stopped between songs and I heard the crashing of waves in the distance. Only House August would be arrogant enough to live so close to the open ocean. New York was different. The city was bordered by rivers and a harbor that were monitored around the clock. This palatial house stared straight at the dark waters like a dare.

I shook off my concerns. I wasn't here to judge the house or its occupant. I was here to rescue him.

Nausea rolled through me at the thought of seeing him again.

"Britt?"

I spun toward the familiar voice. "Roger."

I should've realized the vampire would be here. Roger Akers was the prince's best friend and confidante. He knew where all the bodies were buried, mainly because he was usually the one ordered to bury them—metaphorically speaking, of course. As far as vampires were concerned, Roger was one of the good ones, albeit complicit in his friend's misadventures.

The vampire couldn't hide his shock. "What in the devil are you doing here?" He leaned forward to peck my cheek. As polite and respectful as ever.

"I'm in town on House business and was instructed to stop by and check on the prince." True enough.

Roger grimaced. "I'm sorry. That can't be easy for you."

"It's fine. I'm a professional."

Roger waved a hand toward the crowd. "As you can see, it's the same s-h-i-t, different day."

Roger's refusal to use curse words had always struck me as comical. He was a vampire whose best friend excelled in debauchery, yet he couldn't bring himself to spew profanity. To be fair, he tried his level best to keep the prince on a straight and narrow path, but he failed far more often than he succeeded.

"And where is your princely pal?"

Roger motioned in the direction of the pool. The water was illuminated by lights at the bottom of the pool, although it was hard to see past all the naked bodies. Did nobody in Palm Beach own a swimsuit?

"I didn't realize I'd wandered into an orgy," I remarked.

Roger smirked. "Next time bring protection."

I patted my weapons concealed by my vest. "Wouldn't dream of coming here without it." My gaze skimmed past the array of fleshy dimples.

And there he was.

The royal jackass.

Resentment bubbled to the surface and I fought to control my emotions. I could handle this. He was one vampire and I'd killed dozens of them. I could deal with a simple conversation, however uncomfortable.

He looked much the same, unfortunately. I would've been overjoyed to see a paunch or a thinning hairline but no such luck. Prince Alaric was still the perfect specimen. His medium-brown hair was styled differently. He wore it wavy and slightly disheveled. The ends brushed his collar. His white shirt was unbuttoned at the top, offering a glimpse of his broad chest. A sudden vision flashed in my mind. My head atop that same chest, pretending to listen for a heartbeat that I knew didn't exist. He didn't lack a heart because he was a vampire.

He lacked a heart because he was Alaric.

Anger coiled in the pit of my stomach as a torrent of buried emotions rushed through me. I reminded myself that I was not here to exact punishment. I wasn't a fury sent on a quest for revenge. This was a rescue mission. I was the knight and he was my damsel in distress.

The damsel stood beside the pool. His rapt attention was currently being given to a buxom blonde. Shocker. Naturally his fangs were on full display. It was the vampire equivalent of a male peacock showing off his feathers.

His predatory nature took over as he sensed he was being watched. Although his head remained directed at the blonde, his eyes shifted to the left. To me. It took a second, but I witnessed the exact moment that recognition kicked in. His back straightened and his body rippled with tension.

Good.

"I think he might've spotted you," Roger whispered.

"You've got to be kidding me." Beaming as though delighted, the prince strode toward me with open arms, leaving the blonde alone and confused.

*I know the feeling, sister*, I thought.

"Britt." His arms were around me before I could move and his lips brushed my cheek. "I can't believe this." He drew back to admire me fully. "Roger, can you believe it?"

"Color me shocked and awed," Roger said. "I'll leave you two to get reacquainted." The vampire inched away, giving me a supportive thumbs up as he disappeared in the crowd.

"What brings you to Palm Beach of all places?" the prince asked.

"You."

He hesitated, uncertain whether to laugh off my response as a joke.

I didn't smile. "Not here, Your Highness."

"No problem. As good as you look, I'd follow you anywhere."

I resisted the urge to roll my eyes. Now wasn't the time to mock his come-on lines. "Take me somewhere private. No guards."

His eyes twinkled with mischief. "Blunt as always, I see."

He smiled and waved to his guests as we maneuvered through the crowd toward the house. He couldn't resist placing his hand on the small of my back. I didn't want to make a scene by brushing it away, so I ignored the sensation it triggered. Or tried to.

The blonde glared at me as we passed by. I wasn't sure that my black jumpsuit and serious ponytail suggested a romantic rival, but I understood the sentiment. Alaric had a way of triggering feelings of jealousy and possession. I once told him it was his superpower. He'd laughed and kissed me.

*If that's my superpower, then you are my Kryptonite.*

Liar.

The prince waved the guards away as they approached us. He steered me toward a lavish study. Huge oil paintings with gilded frames. A bust of the prince himself atop a marble column. One good shove and that bust would break into a million tiny pieces. Maybe I shouldn't have left George in the minivan.

"You didn't dress for the party," he said.

"You mean undress."

The prince staggered to the liquor cabinet, which I assumed took pride of place in every room of the house. I was right. He hadn't changed a bit.

"Drink?" he offered.

"No, thank you."

"It's a party. At least one of us should have a drink." He poured dark amber liquid into a glass and swiveled to face me. "Well, isn't this cozy?"

"Look around. Nothing in this room is cozy." I refused to let his close proximity unravel me. If I intended to complete this mission successfully, I needed to get a grip.

The prince swaggered toward me. He slid his free hand past my head and leaned in, effectively pinning me against the wall. "Tell me, Death Bringer. Have you come to kiss me or kill me?"

His voice was feathery soft. Seductive. Forgotten memories stirred and I hated myself for it.

"Can't it be both?"

He stared at me long and hard for a moment. His lips hovered mere inches from mine and I smelled the alcohol on his breath. I also caught the familiar scent of grapefruit and frankincense. *His* scent. I blocked the rush of memories that threatened to surface. There was too much at stake.

Girding my loins, I stared straight back at him. "Why would I come all the way to Palm Beach to kill you?"

A smile tugged at the sides of his mouth. "Ah, but you admit you'd come all this way to kiss me. Interesting."

I bit my lip, annoyed with myself for walking straight into that one. "I'm not having this conversation when you're drunk."

He raised his glass to his lips and drank. "Then I guess you'll have to wait until the party's over."

I smacked the glass from his hand and it crashed to the floor, shattering into fragments. Amber liquid pooled on the floor. Alaric looked at the mess and laughed. At least he was an agreeable drunk. In fact, I'd never seen him truly angry. His good nature was part of his charm. It was also a double-edged sword. His failure to react strongly suggested he cared very little about anything—or anyone.

"I need you to sober up. Now." I curled my fingers around his arm and focused on the blood in his veins.

He tried to wrench his arm away. "Stop. I can feel you in there."

I tightened my grip and continued to concentrate, forming a connection. Slowly and methodically, I separated the alcohol from the blood and flushed it through his body.

"I command you to stop," he ground out.

"By royal decree?" I couldn't resist a mocking tone.

"Yes," he spat.

"Sorry. The queen's command trumps yours."

His green eyes snapped into focus. "The queen? My mother sent you?"

"I'll tell you in a minute." I wanted all the alcohol out of his system before I broke the bad news. He could get drunk again later to dull the pain, but right now I needed him stone cold sober.

He stopped resisting. I tried to keep my focus on the blood and not the fact that I was touching him again after all this time. It wasn't as easy as I'd hoped. I finished and released him.

He dropped into the closest chair, a wingback draped in crushed velvet. It looked comfortable and inviting, just like the prince himself.

"I'm ready for a nap now. Care to join me? It'll be like old times."

Time to alter the course of his life forever just as he'd once done to me. Despite my enmity, I didn't relish the moment.

"Your father's been murdered. Your mother sent me here to escort you back to New York in one piece."

He gaped at me. "You came all the way here to seek revenge? It's a capital offense to lie to a member of the royal household."

"Do you seriously think I'm that petty?" Apparently he did. "Hold on. Your mother gave me this." I pulled the small object from the pocket of my vest.

The prince plucked the object from my hand and hefted it in his palm. "You're serious."

"I told you that. What are you doing?"

He held up the seven-sided die. "My parents and I are the only three who know the exact weight of this." He paused and I caught a glimpse of pain in his eyes. "Only two of us now, I suppose."

"Listen, Your Highness. This part is important. No one can know about your father. *No one*. It's a matter of House security. Your mother hopes I can get you home safely before the news breaks."

"She's worried I'm also a target," he murmured.

"And that you'll become an even greater one when word gets out." House August would be in a weakened state until the prodigal son returned home.

The prince gave me an appraising look. "So you're my knight in shining black leather?"

"Basically."

He allowed himself a mild grin. "My mother knows me well."

"She didn't choose me for my outfits."

"No, of course not. It's how you look in them that matters."

I closed my eyes and drew a deep breath. There was that good nature again, the one that suggested he wasn't overly distressed by the tragic news.

As if reading my mind, his grin evaporated. "I think she's overreacting. I'll simply turn invisible if she fears for my safety."

"Yes, women love to be told they're overreacting. Besides, you can't sustain invisibility for the entire journey." Even older vampires could only maintain their invisible form for a short period of time. Minutes versus hours.

"Fine. Then why not let me shift and fly back to New York on my own?"

"Too dangerous, Your Highness. Butterflies can't fly very high. And you'd be easier to catch. That's why it's just the two of us. We can stay off the beaten track."

This grin was wry and maybe a touch sad. "We have experience with that, don't we?"

I maintained a neutral expression. "Leave the past in the past, Your Highness. It'll make this trip more tolerable for both of us."

His eyes glimmered with amusement. "You keep saying 'Your Highness.' Since when do you call me that?"

"Since I was assigned to come here on royal business. Trust me, I'm no happier about it than you are."

"Quality time alone with you? How could I not be happy about that?"

The prince just learned about the death of his father and a potential threat to his life, yet he was still flirting. Further proof that his libido ran on autopilot.

He cut a glance at the closed door. "I have to tell Roger."

"I'm afraid that's not possible. Your mother said no one can know."

"But he's Roger. He knows everything."

"He can't know this. Not yet. I'm sorry."

The prince rubbed his temples. "Fine. Then what's the plan? I suppose we can't take one of my vehicles. Too easy to track."

"No, and we can't take the train either. And there won't be any five-star accommodations in your imminent future, I can tell you that much."

"I imagine you still have a network from your old life."

I nodded. "I'm hopeful it's still active. I can't exactly call ahead and make a reservation. It'll be trial and error."

His gaze swept the room and I detected a hint of longing in his eyes. He was settled here. Happy. He didn't want to leave. I knew the feeling. I'd been settled and happy once, too, until I was forced to leave my home. Of course the difference was that I was only a girl at the time, a witch with very few options. Alaric was an adult—a vampire—with the world at his disposal. Another reason to despise him.

The prince exhaled softly, resigned to his fate. "When do we leave?"

"Now works for me."

He scoffed. "In case you haven't noticed, I'm hosting a party. I can't up and go in the middle of it. It'll draw too much attention. If you intend to keep this matter quiet, I need to act normal."

"Wouldn't it be considered normal for you to slip away with a woman for the remainder of the evening?"

He didn't smile. "I suppose it would."

"I can't leave you in the middle of a party. It's too risky. For all we know, the group responsible for your father's death have people poised here to kill you, too."

He rubbed the back of his neck. "It stands to reason." He met my gaze. "My mother is safe?"

"She'll be at the compound waiting for you with your favorite bottle of wine." I imagined.

His brow creased. "How do I know that whoever killed my father didn't hire you to kill me? Who better to gain entry to my house than a former lover?"

"I just watched half the population in the Southern Territories gain entrance to your house."

He squinted at me. "I don't hear a denial, Britt."

"Who could I possibly be working for? I've been tethered to your House for years."

He shrugged. "Maybe this is your ticket out of servitude. Take down House August and gain your freedom."

More like preserve House August and gain my freedom.

"There's a key fact you seem to be missing, Your Highness."

He arched an eyebrow. "And what's that?"

I withdrew one of my daggers and pressed the metal blade against his cheek. "If I was hired to kill you, you'd be dead already."

# FOUR

"You can't be serious. We're riding in that?" Prince Alaric stared at the dark green minivan with a curled lip.

"What would you prefer? A limo? Why not just paint a bright red target on the roof of the car and be done with it?"

He sighed.

"You're lucky we have a vehicle at all." I'd been given cash by the queen for incidentals like this, but I had to use it sparingly. A purchase too luxurious would draw attention to us. An ancient minivan, however, wouldn't warrant a passing glance.

I walked to the passenger side and opened the door with a slight bow. "Your carriage awaits, my liege."

Reluctantly he climbed inside.

I settled behind the wheel and started the car.

"Do you even know how to drive?" he asked.

"I have experience."

"I suppose you would."

"I traveled extensively once upon a time."

"Until you...What was the reason again? I don't think you ever told me the details."

"No, I didn't." I removed my phone and attached it to the charger.

"Wait. Why can you have a phone when you told me not to bring mine?"

"Because someone might be able to track us with yours. No one can do that with mine."

He folded his arms. "Service is notoriously bad in the Southern Territories. Too much satellite disruption."

"I'll take my chances." Dysfunctional satellites and an uprooted earth basically killed off the internet but phones managed to survive. Unfortunately service was patchy and unreliable everywhere. Most of the time I didn't need it in New York. If Olis needed to communicate with me, he had other methods.

The prince grunted. "As stubborn as ever, I see."

I gunned the engine. "Welcome aboard. This is your captain speaking. I intend to get us as far as Atlanta today. Since the roads probably haven't been paved since before the Great Eruption, we could be in for a bumpy ride so buckle up."

He arched an eyebrow. "You're my captain now? Why not drive straight through Atlanta? If we take turns, one can drive while the other sleeps."

"We can't drive straight up the main highway to New York. It's too obvious."

"But the slower we go, the more risk we take on."

"Even if we stuck to the highway most of the way, we'd have to take a detour through Virginia and Maryland."

Understanding flashed in the vampire's eyes. "Won't that also be obvious? I still think we should surprise them and drive straight up the highway. No one would dare follow us through Monster Maze."

"I'm not avoiding one risk of death by dropping you straight into another."

"Every day there's a risk of death, Britt. You know that better than most."

My hands tightened on the wheel at the mention of my name. His voice seemed to linger on it, caress it. Gods, why did he have this effect on me? No one I'd met before or after had left an impression on me like the vampire prince. I forced myself to stay focused on the job. Deliver the prince home and gain my freedom. A couple rough days and this would all be over.

George's head poked between the seats. I'd been so focused on the prince that I'd forgotten the dragon was there.

The vampire took one look at George and groaned. "You didn't mention your toy dragon would be joining us."

"You know he doesn't like being called a toy."

"I don't know how you can tell what he likes. He can't talk."

"Never stopped us from knowing." I winced at my own response. The past was spilling out of me. I had to put the emotional dam back in place.

I felt the vampire's gaze on me, but I refused to give him the satisfaction of turning. I kept my attention on the dark road ahead.

"George, please stay in the back," I ordered. "I can't afford any distractions."

The prince turned to address the dragon. "That's right, George. I'm more than enough of a distraction for her."

I wasn't prepared for how it would feel to be alone in a vehicle with him. The proximity in closed quarters was killing me.

"Tell me what you've been up to," he said, making himself comfortable.

"Put your seatbelt on," I advised.

He chuckled. "I'm a vampire, Britt. I don't need a seatbelt."

"If we have an accident, you can still sustain a serious injury. You can also be beheaded. My minivan. My rules."

Begrudgingly he snapped the seatbelt into place. "I forgot how bossy you are."

"Seems to me it was one of the qualities you liked about me."

"Only in the bedroom." He paused. "Or the hot tub. Or the alley behind the compound."

I cut him off before he mentioned every single place we ever had sex. "I get the idea."

"You gave me lots of ideas. You were very creative."

"Just stop talking."

He turned his gaze to the window. "I'm going to miss the beach. I met a gorgeous siren called Lois there."

"Congratulations."

"The beach is one of the few places you and I didn't christen. Care to pull over and tick it off the list?"

I ignored him. "If you're going to proposition me the entire way back to New York, I may just hand you over to your enemies now and save my sanity."

He tilted back his head and laughed. "Gods, I've missed you. Nobody else dares to speak to me the way you do."

"Nobody else can kill you without touching you."

He turned his head to observe me. "How's the city? Is that taco stand still there?"

"Yes. I can't get guacamole if my life depended on it, but I've accepted my fate."

"Avocados are hard to come by everywhere. It takes a lot

of magic to grow them and nobody wants to dedicate resources to them."

"I know the reason. I was complaining for the sake of it. There's a shipment due in and now I'll miss it."

He rubbed his temple. "I can't believe House Nilsson would stoop to this level. We have a truce."

"How do you know it's them?"

"I don't, but they're the most obvious choice. They have the most to gain from a weakened House August."

"But you have a truce, like you said. Are they the type to violate it?" King Stefan and Queen Margot lived in the Midwest. Their compound was located at the former Mall of America in Minneapolis. The Houses had clashed over territory before, but they seemed to have resolved their differences for the time being.

"Did Mother send a note with you?"

I shook my head. "Putting something in writing is too dangerous."

"*You're* too dangerous, but she still sent you."

We lapsed into a silence that stretched all the way to the outskirts of Atlanta. I kept my eyes on the road and watched for any roadblocks or signs of an ambush. It was hard to strategize without knowing the identity of the opponent, which was likely one reason they hadn't claimed responsibility. The element of surprise gave them an advantage.

The prince whistled, snapping me out of my trance. "What happened here?"

I followed his gaze out the window. Atlanta wasn't the wasteland that Monster Maze was, but it wasn't a paradise either. Much of the city had been razed by a horde of dragons about twenty years ago. The creatures had taken a liking to the area and chose to nest there. A second dragon species decided they'd like to call Atlanta home, too, and a battle between the two hordes left the sprawling city in shambles. The dragons fought until there were very few left alive on either side. The remaining dragons chose to relocate but the damage was done. Vampires didn't want to live in such an undesirable hellhole, so the area was taken over by a variety of different species. The Falcon Pack, a group of werewolves that named themselves after a pre-Eternal Night football team, were the strongest faction. The Sunshine Coven was also headquartered here. They were one of the many covens that rejected me early on when I had nowhere to go. My magic was considered "unclean," as though I had any control over the type of magic I inherited. I could no more change my magic than I could change the color of my eyes. I opted not to hold a grudge and found another use for my magic instead. I became an assassin. A survivor.

"Haven't you seen Atlanta before?" I asked, turning right at a defunct traffic light.

Slowly he shook his head. "The train passes through so quickly, I've never noticed the landscape. Too dark."

"Well, here's your chance for an up-close-and-personal look." I pulled onto a dirt road and traveled another mile until we reached a stone house. Smoke wafted from the chimney and blended with the darkness. Good, they were home.

I parked the minivan in front of the garage and unbuckled my seatbelt. "Listen closely. Your name is Jerry. You and I are dating, but your family doesn't approve. You're old-fashioned. We're traveling west to seek the blessing of your aunt before you propose."

Prince Alaric stared at me blankly. "Jerry? Do I look like a Jerry to you?"

"Fine. Be Paul or Ringo. I don't care. Just stick to the story, whatever happens."

He drummed his fingers on the passenger door. "What about Rafe? That's a good name. Sexy and strong." He looked at me expectantly.

"I think we should choose something that accurately reflects you."

He scowled. "Very funny."

"What about Colin?"

He slouched against the seat. "Do I need to be Colin the entire way home? I'm quite attached to my name."

"It's preferable to being killed, isn't it?" I opened the driver's side door and stretched my legs.

Alaric remained seated, eyeing the house. "Who lives here?"

"I'm not entirely sure. I know who I expect to live here, but we've been out of touch for years."

The vampire glanced in the direction of the house. "What if you're wrong? Should I stay hidden until we know for certain?"

"That's the plan."

I left him inside the minivan. George took the opportunity to stretch his wings outside. I withdrew a dagger from my utility belt and pricked the skin of my palm. As I walked around the minivan, I dripped blood and performed an incantation to ward the vehicle. No one would be able to get to the prince while I was inside. The basic ward wouldn't last forever, but it would hold long enough to allow me a conversation with the home's occupants.

My steps along the walkway were slow and casual. I didn't want to appear to be in a hurry in case anyone was watching.

I gripped the brass knocker and gave it three deliberate whacks against the door.

"Who's there?" a gruff voice called from the other side of the door. He sounded older than fifty, the right age group.

"I'm looking for an old friend."

"Does this friend have a name?"

"Immortal, though not a vampire. Food of the gods, though not to be tasted."

The door opened, revealing a stout man with a thick mustache and an impressive head of salt-and-pepper hair. "By anyone other than his wife, of course." He broke into a broad smile. "Britt, my dear girl, look at you."

"Hello, Ambrose."

The wizard observed me from head to toe. "You're alive. What a miracle." He turned away from the door. "Joan, you must come and see who's here. You might want to bring your smelling salts."

I'd first met Ambrose and Joan following my rejection by the Sunshine Coven. They'd caught the closing credits of my fight against three werewolves in a park and invited me home for supper and to tend to my wounds. I stayed three weeks. Although the couple possessed acceptable forms of magic, they declined to join any particular group. History had taught Ambrose that safety in numbers was a lie, so he opted to live a life outside the norm and Joan was happy to join him. I'd visited a half dozen times since then, usually seeking refuge before or after a job in the Southern Territories. I was pleased to see they were still alive and together.

Joan looked older, too. The lines across her forehead and around her mouth had deepened. Once reviled among humans, wrinkles were now the welcome markers of a long life. They were the human equivalent of silver hair on a vampire. Both were worn with a deep sense of pride.

"We haven't seen you in such a long time," Joan said. "We thought something awful might've happened."

"In your line of work, it's almost inevitable," Ambrose added.

They had no moral or ethical objection to my line of work—as long as I was only killing vampires.

"There was an incident a few years back. I ended up in an unpleasant predicament."

Ambrose held out his arms. "And here you are, living to tell the tale."

"Only because I sold out."

Joan's eyes narrowed. "Sold out. What does that mean, dear?"

"I've been working security for House August. It was that or be executed." I shrugged. "I didn't love my options."

Ambrose cast a glance over my shoulder and seemed to notice the minivan outside. "Have you brought a friend?"

"About that..." I drew a breath. "He's a vampire. We need a place to lay low to sleep and eat. We'll be out of your hair in a few hours, I promise."

Ambrose and Joan exchanged glances. "Is he a friend of yours?" Joan asked. She didn't sound convinced.

"Yes, a very special friend." I couldn't tell them the truth. It would put them at risk as well as Alaric. "His name is Colin." I gave them the spiel about traveling west.

Joan clapped her hands. "Oh, how wonderful. I have to be honest, dear, I never expected you to settle down with anyone, least of all a vampire."

"Don't leave him stranded outside," Ambrose added. "Bring him in so we can take the measure of him."

I said a silent prayer that Alaric behaved himself. I didn't want to put anyone in an awkward position.

I retrieved the prince from the minivan and reminded him to say as little as possible during our stay. We entered the house and the aroma of stew filled my nostrils.

"I suppose I could stand to be Colin for one meal," the prince said in a quiet voice.

I found the couple in the kitchen. Ambrose stirred a pot on the stove while Joan chopped carrots.

"Joan. Ambrose. This is Colin."

The vampire bowed. "Thank you for your kindness."

"No trouble at all," Ambrose said.

Joan carried the cutting board to the pot and swept in the carrots.

"You still have your vegetable garden out back, I take it?"

"Oh, yes." Joan's head bobbed as she returned the cutting board to the island. "It's small, but it's served us well all these years. Just enough magic to sustain it, but not so much as to attract unwanted attention."

I silenced the prince with a deadly look. This wasn't the time to punish anyone for using magic, certainly not when they were only using it to grow vegetables to feed themselves.

Joan seemed to remember she was in the presence of a vampire because her skin faded to the shade of a white peach.

Alaric quickly attempted to put her at ease. "I'm not the magic police. I have no desire to report you to House August."

My stomach unclenched. This ruse was going to be harder than I thought.

"Can I offer you a drink or a snack?" Joan offered. "I'm

afraid I don't have any blood." Her fingers moved to touch her neck. She seemed to remember he could drink straight from the tap.

"Not to worry. Britt already thought of that and packed some for me," Alaric said, beaming at me with false pride. "She thinks of everything."

"She's very smart, our Britt," Ambrose agreed.

"I'll have water," I said, eager to move off the topic of me.

"The stew will be a couple hours," Joan said. "Why don't we pack a small picnic and enjoy it down by the pond? It's been ages since Ambrose and I have done that."

"Sounds lovely," Alaric said.

"Has it been checked recently?" I asked. Bodies of water were tricky in a post-Great Eruption world. Even the most innocuous-looking pond could house any number of water-based creatures. I once fought off a kelpie that grabbed my ankle with its teeth and tried to pull me to a watery grave. It wasn't unusual to read about a boat full of fishermen being carted off by a kraken. The East and Hudson Rivers had more than their share of stories, too.

"A few days ago," Ambrose said. "But we've never had any uninvited occupants so I doubt they'll suddenly show up today."

"Where did you two meet?" Joan asked as she bustled around the kitchen gathering an assortment of items for the picnic basket.

Alaric placed a hand on my shoulder and squeezed. "Where all the best couples meet, naturally."

"Church," I said.

Joan and Ambrose laughed uncomfortably.

"She's teasing, obviously," Alaric said. "We met at a tavern in New York. You know what a barfly our Britt is.

She looked so sexy in her black leather pants and white top, I couldn't take my eyes off her. Then she ordered a bourbon smash and I knew it was kismet."

A lump formed in my throat when I realized he was describing our actual first meeting, right down to the outfit. How on earth did he remember those details?

"What was so special about the drink?" Ambrose asked.

"It's one of my favorites and only one tavern in the whole city knows how to make it properly."

"The one where you met?" Joan asked eagerly.

He aimed a finger at her. "The very one. We became inseparable after that."

"You don't mind that she's tethered to House August? Limits your options if you can't pick up and go wherever you like," Ambrose said.

"I had to beg the king and queen to give her time off for this journey as a personal favor," Alaric told them, warming to the story. "My parents have a history with the royal family, which helped."

Joan recoiled slightly. "Oh, I see."

"Time to walk," Ambrose said. "You've been cooped up in a car for hours. It'll feel good to stretch those legs."

"I'm always up for a little exercise." Anything to end this conversation. Alaric was enjoying himself a bit too much.

We exited the house via the back door and Alaric made a show of breathing deeply. "It's wonderful to be in the countryside again."

Joan laughed. "I don't think I often hear the Atlanta suburbs referred to as the countryside."

"When you grow up in New York, everything else feels like the countryside," Alaric replied. "Isn't that right, dumpling?"

Dumpling?

"Britt didn't grow up in the city," Ambrose pointed out. "From what I hear, Lancaster is as rural as it gets these days."

"Lancaster," Alaric repeated blankly.

"Don't you know where she's originally from?" Ambrose wagged a finger at him. "Seems like you should do less talking and more listening in your relationship."

Alaric studied me. "Yes, it seems so."

"I don't know if it counts as a place I grew up when I left there at age seven." I said 'left' as though the decision had been voluntary. I couldn't bear to be more honest than that. Alaric had already discarded me like trash. No reason to tell him that entire covens treated me the same way. He'd only think even less of me.

Not that his opinion mattered. I'd shaken off that need for acceptance years ago.

Alaric surveyed the landscape. "I can't believe how flat the land is here."

"I'm surprised you can see any of it," Joan said. "We don't get much light in this area. House August doesn't want to invest in the infrastructure in these parts."

"Why not?" the prince asked.

"You'd have to ask them," Ambrose interjected. "I suspect it's because they don't live here and, therefore, don't care."

"That's rather harsh," Alaric commented.

"Almost there," Joan sang out, swinging the basket.

We arrived at an area that was the epitome of scorched earth. It was rare that the ground was even blacker than the air around us. A strong sense of foreboding overcame me. I stopped at the edge, unwilling to go further.

"What is this place?"

Alaric pivoted toward Ambrose. "Dragons?"

"Yes and no," Ambrose said. "The black ash is thanks to dragons. The rest is the handiwork of the Angels of Mercy. A nice name for a terrible group."

"Terrible depends on your perspective, darling."

"Who are the Angels of Mercy?" I asked.

"I'm surprised you haven't heard of them in your travels. They're sometimes called the Pey," Ambrose said.

"The Great Eruption?" I asked, which was shorthand for 'are they monsters?'

The wizard shook his head. "No. Like our vampire overlords, the Pey lived in the shadows for centuries during the time of humans."

"Overlords?" Alaric echoed.

Ambrose's cheeks reddened. "I meant no offense, Colin. Simply stating a fact."

"When vampires ascended, the Pey tagged along for the ride," Joan chimed in.

"The Pey are nothing but scavengers," Alaric told me. "They survive on the blood and flesh of the dying."

"That's what I meant about perspective," Joan said. "In times of war, the Pey helped end the misery of soldiers dying a slow and painful death on the battlefield, which is how they earned their nickname."

"Mercy killing," I murmured.

"They've actually suffered greatly during the Eternal Night," Alaric added. "You would think they would've flourished given their relationship to our species, but with the wars of men raging all the time, the Pey have been unable to sustain their numbers and their population has declined."

"Small mercies," Ambrose remarked.

I examined the concave clearing. "Is that what happened here? The Pey picked off the dying?"

"When the first horde of dragons arrived, people flocked here for shelter."

"This area was still part of a forest then," I said, more to myself.

Ambrose nodded. "The people attacked the dragons as they flew overhead and the dragons responded in kind. The dragons burned the forest to the ground and all who sought refuge here."

"And the Pey seized an opportunity to feed," Alaric said without a trace of the disgust I felt.

"It's been said that you could hear the screams from Charleston," Joan said.

"I don't care what anybody claims," Ambrose said. "There's nothing merciful about being savaged by a monster during your final moments."

I wrapped my arms around myself and blocked the image of the suffering that occurred here.

Joan's gaze flicked to me. "That's enough unpleasant chatter for one day."

"Speaking of dragons, I think I might spy a friend of yours," Ambrose said, pointing behind me.

I twisted to see George's silhouette careening toward us. The pygmy dragon narrowly missed flying straight into the back of Alaric's head.

"We're having appetizers," I explained.

George seemed keen on the idea. He hovered above as we set up our picnic beside the pond and enjoyed slices of apple with peanut butter, as well as carrot sticks and cucumber.

"Ambrose makes peanut butter with the peanuts from his own farm," I boasted.

"Impressive," Alaric murmured. I got the sense he wasn't a fan of peanuts.

"George can roast them for you if you like," I suggested.

"I think I'll wait for the stew," the prince replied.

I bit back a smile.

Joan rose to her feet, her knees cracking along the way. She seemed so much older than when I last saw her. "Why don't we head back to the house and enjoy our supper by the fire?"

"No arguments from me." Alaric patted his stomach. "I'm looking forward to a hot meal."

Unsurprising given that his last meal probably consisted solely of blood and alcohol.

As we trekked back to the house, I watched for any signs of trouble. I was relieved when we arrived without incident. If someone was tracking Alaric, I'd do my best to make sure they had a helluva time finding him.

Dinner was pleasant enough, although I felt guilty for the lies I was forced to tell. I kept the conversation to a minimum, despite their attempts to make friendly inquiries about our relationship. I knew they weren't being nosy and actually cared, which made the situation that much harder. It was incredibly rare that anybody interrogated me about my personal life, especially because they were happy for me. Liam was the only one and his inquiries were more gossip-driven than anything else.

After dinner Joan made up a mattress in the spare room. There was no point in objecting. The vampire and I were supposedly madly in love and I had to play the part. Besides, I wasn't about to leave him alone behind a closed door where I didn't have eyes on him. For better or worse, we were attached at the hip.

"You sleep," I ordered, once we were alone in the room. "I'll take first watch."

"Do you really think that's necessary?" He smoothed the sheet beside him. "It's small, but if we stack our bodies, we can make it work. If I recall correctly, you prefer being on top."

I kicked the side of his leg in protest. The vampire rolled on top of me with preternatural speed and pinned my body beneath his.

"You're angry, I get it, but do not forget yourself. I am still a prince and you still belong to our House. To me." He remained pressed against me, a smirk beginning to form.

Big mistake.

I head-butted that smirk right off his face. His head snapped back, more a result of surprise than force.

"I am not your property," I ground out. "I am Britt the Bloody, tasked with carting your sorry ass to New York. And if you ever put your hands on me again uninvited, I will empty your veins and leave your carcass for the Pey."

Smiling, he rubbed his wounded forehead. "Uninvited suggests there might be an invitation forthcoming."

I groaned and swiveled toward the mattress. "Change of plans. You're taking first watch."

He slid to a seated position against the wall, facing the mattress. "Excellent. If you recall, I like to watch."

I didn't reward him with a response. I simply tugged the sheet over my head and went to sleep.

# FIVE

I never failed to leave the cozy stone house without feeling rested and sated. It was a comfort to know that not all good things came to an end.

The prince and I slipped out while our hosts were asleep. It was easier to leave without conversation. We were less likely to reveal more than we should.

I whistled softly for George.

"I think that went well," Alaric said, sliding behind the wheel of the minivan.

I held open the door. "What do you think you're doing?"

"My turn to drive."

"I don't think so."

"If I drive, you're better able to protect me in an ambush. If your hands are occupied, you can't hold your weapons."

Damn. I hated when he made a good point.

I walked to the other side of the minivan and slid open the back door for George. The pygmy dragon sailed inside spraying dirt everywhere.

"Seriously, George. Let's try to keep it relatively clean for the short time we'll be using it." I climbed into the passenger seat and buckled my seatbelt. "Ready when you are."

The prince inclined his head toward the house. "Are you sure you don't want to wake them to say good-bye?"

I shook my head. "I don't do good-byes."

He started the minivan. "And here I thought we were nothing alike."

"Go left," I instructed when he reached the end of the dirt road.

"But we came from the right."

"Exactly. We're not retracing our steps."

"Don't we want to rejoin the road?"

"We'll join a different road." I reached across and jerked the wheel to the left. It was then that I noticed the fuel gage and felt a rush of gratitude. Ambrose and Joan must've filled the tank while we slept. They were better people than I'd ever be.

Alaric begrudgingly turned left and hit the gas.

"Not too fast," I warned. "You don't want to draw attention to us."

"We want to get to New York as quickly as possible, don't we? The sooner we get there, the sooner we can go our separate ways and you can stop shooting daggers out of your eyes."

"If I could shoot daggers out of my eyes, you'd be dead a thousand times over by now."

The prince didn't heed my warning about his speed. It wasn't that a vampire patrol would pull us over for speeding—there were no limits anymore. No road rules at all, really, except don't cause property damage and don't kill anyone. The rules were easier to abide in an Eternal

Night world given that heavy traffic was a relic of the past.

We reached a five-point intersection and I told Alaric to take a right.

"Why? Straight looks good."

"I don't know the route if we go straight. I know it if we take the road to the right."

"Live a little," he said, and continued straight across the intersection.

In the backseat, George grunted. I turned to look at the dragon. "I know, buddy. I'm sorry. The prince is a stubborn ox with a death wish."

"It's been years since you took the route you claim to know. It's probably changed five times since you last saw it."

"Fine. Have it your way." *You usually do.* Two circles of faint yellow light appeared in the sideview mirror and I straightened.

"Relax," Alaric said. "We're not going to be the only vehicle on the road, although ours may be the only vehicle from 1986."

I ignored the jibe and kept my focus on the headlights. We couldn't be complacent. There was no way of knowing whether this would be a fellow traveler or an assassination attempt.

I removed Monster Masher from its hiding place and held the gun against the door, low enough so that it wouldn't be visible to any car that pulled alongside us.

Alaric cut a sideways glance at me and noticed the gun. "That side piece is almost as pretty as mine."

I glared at him. "You'd better be talking about a gun."

Grinning, he returned his gaze to the road ahead. "Sure, let's go with that."

The headlights drew closer. Alaric was driving too fast

as it was. If this vehicle was gaining on us, they had to be flooring it.

"George, I may need you," I told the dragon. "Get ready." The windows were electric. I hit the button to make sure mine worked. You could never be sure with electric. It wasn't as unreliable as more advanced technology, but it wasn't perfect either.

The window opened a crack, enough to let in a cool burst of air and, more importantly, fit the snub nose of the Monster Masher.

Now that the vehicle was closer, I recognized the silhouette of a truck. From the boxy shape, it was likely an old Army truck. Not good news.

Alaric glanced in the rearview mirror. "How did they find us?"

"I don't know that anyone found us. It could be highway robbers."

"Then I'll just tell them who I am and send them on their merry way."

"Have you lost your mind? You can't do that. You're Colin until we reach New York."

"Then they'll try to kill us."

"We don't know who they are. They might try to kill us anyway." 'Try' was the important word in that sentence.

The truck was nearly alongside us now. They were driving too close to simply be passing us. They were marauding pirates preparing to board our ship.

It was time to send a message.

"George, now!" I craned my neck to see the window was still intact. "What are you waiting for?"

The dragon's claws scraped the panel of controls on the door. The button wasn't working.

"Hurry, I need firepower!"

The dragon whined as the truck became fully visible. I was right about the Army truck. I counted only one occupant, the driver. There were likely more piled in the back.

Frantic, I glanced at my controls.

"It's the child safety lock," Alaric said. "You need to unlock it on your panel." He sounded remarkably calm under the circumstances.

"Why did they ever need child safety locks? Were children anxious to hurl themselves from a moving vehicle?" I was meant to be the one who remained cool under pressure. Alaric's presence was wreaking havoc on my professional prowess.

Still holding the Monster Masher, I hit the unlock button with my elbow and George's window slid all the way down just as the truck pulled flush against the minivan.

The pygmy dragon didn't wait for a command. He unloaded a stream of firepower at the truck. Wheels squealed as the truck jerked to the right and nearly ran off the road.

I lowered my window and fired at the front tire. Bullseye. The truck skidded to a halt on the side of the road.

"Pull over," I ordered.

"Shouldn't we keep driving?"

"So they can catch up to us again later? No, I'm putting an end to this right now."

Alaric did as instructed.

"Stay here. Do not leave this minivan. George, you're with me." I opened the back door and released the dragon.

Together we ventured toward the truck. There was no sign of movement.

I took careful steps across the road with the Monster Masher poised for action. The side of the truck was partially melted and the tire now featured a gaping hole.

The resale value had decreased dramatically in a matter of minutes.

The window slid down and a voice called, "Don't shoot! Not bullets or fire or insults. Not anything that might hurt me." The driver's door opened and a vampire emerged.

My hand dropped to my side. "Roger?"

With a hesitant smile, the vampire offered an awkward wave. "Hey, you guys. Fancy seeing you here on a deserted back road in the middle of nowhere."

Alaric must've been watching from the safety of the minivan because he was by my side in a nanosecond. "How the devil did you find us?"

"Funny story." Roger rubbed the back of his neck. "I tracked you here."

"Tracked me how? I wasn't allowed to bring my phone."

"Right. You see, I tagged you a while back..."

Frown lines appeared on Alaric's forehead. "Tagged me?"

"Yes, as a security measure. Remember when you got drunk and went home with that mermaid and she tried to drown you in the hot tub?"

"I understand the sentiment," I muttered.

"I vaguely recall," Alaric said.

"After that, I was determined nothing like that would ever happen again, so I hired a wizard to make a locator charm for you."

Alaric's eyes popped with fury. "You did what?"

"I know, I know. I was being overly cautious, but you have no idea what it's like to...look after you."

"I'm not a toddler," Alaric said in a clipped tone.

"I realize that, but when I saw how far you'd traveled..." Roger's face grew flushed. "And you'd shown up out of nowhere, Britt. No offense but between your personal history and your romantic history, I was concerned by his sudden disappearance."

I didn't blame him. I would've felt the same in his position.

"Why are you here in the Land That Time Forgot?" Roger asked. "More importantly, why are you here together?"

I ignored his questions. "Where did you get an Army truck?"

"I bought it to transport alcohol between the warehouse and the estate. You'd be surprised how many times I've nearly been robbed."

"Who else can access this charm?" I asked.

"No one," Roger said quickly. "I swear. I'm the only one who knows about it." He paused. "And the wizard who made it, but he didn't know who I was making it for. He didn't even know my name."

Alaric patted his pockets. "Where's the charm?"

Roger tapped behind his own ear.

"We need to destroy it," I said.

Alaric touched the skin behind his ear. "It's so small, I can barely feel it."

"That's what she said," Roger joked.

Alaric didn't crack a smile. He removed the tiny charm and gazed at it in the palm of his hand. "How do we destroy it?"

George flapped his wings in a bid for attention.

Alaric looked at him askance. "I'm not getting my hand burnt to a crisp just so we can destroy the charm."

"You don't have to hold it, genius. Toss it in the air." I pivoted to the dragon. "Heads up, George. Ready. Aim."

The prince did as instructed.

I pointed to the tiny object in the air. "Fire!"

George let loose a stream of fire and the charm disintegrated.

"Team work makes the dream work," Roger quipped. He raised his hand for a fist bump, but Alaric ignored it.

"You and I will talk about this later," the prince said.

"So can I ask where you're going?"

"No," Alaric and I said in unison.

"Wait. Are you two running off to elope?" Beaming, Roger clapped his hands. "I always suspected you two were meant for each other. Even after you broke up with her, I told myself, 'Roger, your best friend is a moron. He's never going to meet anyone like Britt. She's the only one who can keep him in line.'"

Roger didn't know how wrong he was.

"Wherever you decide to go," Roger continued rambling, "steer clear of Toledo. There are reports of unusual werewolf activity."

"Like a stage production of A Chorus Line?" I asked. The werewolves I knew wouldn't be caught dead in a musical.

Roger's brow furrowed. "Like entire packs fighting to the death over border disputes."

That didn't sound unusual to me. Packs fought over territory all the time.

"We're not eloping," Alaric said.

"We're not together," I added. "Not in the romantic sense."

Roger's expression crumpled. "Oh. Right. I'm sorry. Forget everything I just said." He gestured to me. "You don't have a spell for memory loss, do you? Because I could really use that right now. For all of us."

I couldn't help but smile. "I'm afraid that's not in my

wheelhouse, but maybe you can try your wizard contact when you get back to Palm Beach."

Roger's eyebrows inched up. "You're sending me back? How? You've destroyed my mode of transport."

"You can't come with us," I said. "We'll drop you somewhere, but you need to go back to Palm Beach."

Roger's gaze darted from Alaric to me. "I don't like this. Something is off."

The prince kept his expression neutral. It seemed his talent for deception was coming in handy. "The truth is I'm returning to New York. I didn't want to tell you because I knew you'd insist on coming and I wanted time alone with Britt. That's why we're not taking the train. The time would pass too quickly." He reached for my hand. "I was hoping this trip would reignite our passion for one another."

Roger laughed. "I don't think a lack of passion was ever the problem. Don't you remember? You told me Britt was the hottest s-e-x you ever had and you wished she was a vampire so you could..."

Alaric coughed loudly. "That's quite enough, Roger."

I suppressed a smile, although I would've liked to hear the end of that sentence.

Alaric clapped his friend on the shoulder. "I appreciate you looking out for me, I really do, but I'm ordering you to return to Palm Beach. Someone needs to be in charge during my absence and I'd like that someone to be you."

"How long will you be in New York?"

"Not sure. I'll send word to you when I get there."

Roger glanced at the minivan. "Would you mind if I napped in the back while you find a place to drop me? I've been driving for hours and I'm pretty beat."

"George will make room for you."

We settled into the minivan and resumed our journey.

If I recalled correctly, there was a branch line out this way that joined the main railroad where Roger could board the Silver Meteor to Palm Beach.

True to his word, Roger fell asleep within minutes. George regarded the vampire with a watchful eye.

"I can't believe he tracked me all the way here," Alaric murmured.

"That's what I call a best friend." George would do the same for me, I knew it in my bones.

After another hour, my stomach gurgled loud enough to attract Alaric's attention.

"Time to stop?" he asked.

Roger poked his head between the seats. "Stop where? There's nothing for miles. It's like you're actively trying to avoid civilization."

Alaric and I exchanged looks.

The prince pulled off the road and parked. "Should we send George out to hunt?"

Roger stared out the windshield at the block of trees to our left. "A real forest. How about that? There must be a coven nearby."

"Not that I know of," I said. It was rare that a forest sustained itself without the aid of magic, but it happened. Nobody could explain why or how. Without the sun, it shouldn't be possible.

George flapped his wings above us.

"Must be nice to travel with a portable grill," Roger joked.

I stretched my arms over my head. "George is multi-talented."

Alaric sniffed the air. "I smell smoke."

As a vampire, his senses were superior to mine. "Forest fire or campfire?"

"How do I tell the difference?"

"Is it faint?" I asked.

"It could be faint because it's far away," Roger said.

Before we settled on an answer, the pygmy dragon flew through the trees to investigate.

My hands flew to my hips. "George!"

He didn't return.

Great. Now I had to go.

"You two stay in the minivan," I said. "I'll check it out."

"I'm not letting you charge through the forest by yourself," Alaric shot back. "You have no idea what's in there."

"There's safety in numbers," Roger added with a shrug.

I debated the options. The better choice was to load everybody into the minivan and keep driving. George would find us eventually.

On the other hand, what if it was a forest fire? Maybe there was something we could do to stop it. The world couldn't afford to lose more trees, certainly not ones that managed to survive the Eternal Night.

"Fine, let's go," I said, and entered the forest.

The trees were a mixture of maple, oak, and birch. The combination of scents took me straight back to my childhood. I was six years old, wandering through the forest in Lancaster and exploring nature. Watching a caterpillar crawl across a leaf. Using a stick as a sword as I pretended to fight with my friend Dina. Listening to the birdsong as I skipped back to the enclave. I'd loved every minute of it—until the day my magic was discovered. I shut down the memories. There was no point in remembering them. All they did was remind me of the pain I'd felt upon being expelled. I was Eve, cast out of the Garden of Eden forever.

The smell of smoke intensified as we arrived at a clearing. Not a forest fire then. George was nowhere to be seen.

A solitary figure stood in front of an open fire. Dressed in a black cloak and a black mask, they would have been invisible against the dark backdrop of the forest if not for the orange and red flames that illuminated them.

They dropped a sturdy branch on the ground as we approached and edged away from the fire.

I held up my hands in a placating gesture. "We won't hurt you. We're just passing through. We smelled the smoke and came to investigate."

"I, too, am passing through. I am but a simple traveler." The figure removed the mask to reveal an old woman. Her white hair was cut short, which made her wrinkles more noticeable.

"In ancient times a simple traveler was usually a god in disguise," I remarked. "Are you sure you're not Athena or Hera?"

The woman smiled and I noticed the row of rotted teeth. "You know your history."

"Not history," Alaric interjected. "Myth. Folklore." He motioned to the mask in her hand. "What's with the costume?"

"Not a costume. It was once a ceremonial helmet but parts have been worn away over the years." She gazed at the mask. "It's made of gold if you can believe it."

The metal had turned dull and discolored, which was probably for the best. If she crossed paths with the wrong people, they'd relieve her of her treasure without hesitation.

"What's the ceremony?" Roger asked.

The old woman set the mask on a log. "A celebration of gratitude for another day lived."

I didn't blame her for celebrating. Based on her appearance, I'd say she won the life lottery.

"I'm Britt and this is Colin and Roger." To my relief,

Roger didn't comment on the use of a fake name for the prince.

"I'm Elana."

"Nice to meet you, Elana. This forest is beautiful. I'm glad it's only you we smelled and not a forest fire."

The old woman looked around as though noticing her surroundings for the first time. "These woods are ancient. The trees have their own magic to sustain them."

Alaric snorted. "Magic trees? Nonsense. There must be a coven nearby that acts as a caretaker."

The woman observed him like he was an ant on her loaf of fresh bread. "There is no coven attached to this forest. The witches don't like it here."

"Why not?"

She shrugged. "Because I am here."

Alaric laughed, assuming it was a joke, but I knew better. Vampires might excel in the five senses, but I excelled in the sixth. There was something about her—a quiet strength. Magical energy hummed just below the pruned surface.

"You said you were a traveler," Roger pointed out.

"And do you know how large this forest is? It takes days to travel from one part to another."

"You use the term loosely," Roger muttered.

"Would you mind if we shared your fire, Elana?" Alaric asked. "Britt could do with a little warmth and a cooked meal."

The woman spread her arms. "You are most welcome, although I don't believe you need my fire when you travel with your own."

I turned to see George flying into the clearing. The pygmy dragon clutched something long between his jaws. He swooped low and dropped it straight into the flames.

"I believe that's your meal," Alaric said.

"It'll burn to a crisp," I said.

With expert precision, Elana stepped on the end of a stick and sent it sailing through the air into her outstretched hand.

"I think she may have done that once or twice before," Roger whispered.

The old woman used the stick to retrieve the offering from the fire. A snake. I'd eaten worse. She held the snake a reasonable distance from the fire and turned it occasionally to fully cook it.

"Thank you," I said.

We settled around the fire like numbers on a clock. Alaric and Roger sat on either side of me at five and seven, respectively, with Elana seated at nine. George continued his exploration by flying around the clearing, occasionally stopping on a branch above us.

"Look for chestnuts," I called to the dragon. "Those are good roasted." I preferred nuts to snake, not that I was in a position to be selective.

Elana cast an admiring glance at the dragon's departing figure. "You're very fortunate to have a companion like that. Fire is worshipped now more than ever." She tore a piece of snake meat from the stick and shoved it into her mouth, chewing audibly. Impeccable manners on this one.

"I don't know if worship is the right word," Alaric countered.

Elana cast him a sidelong glance. "You don't spend much time outside city walls, do you, vampire?"

She was right. He didn't. Even in Palm Beach, he was surrounded by a civilization he understood. Vampires and those who benefitted from their relationship with vampires.

"It's not a surprise," I remarked. "Any form of light is like an act of rebellion."

Alaric grunted. "Light is only necessary for the…" He caught himself before he finished the insult.

"For what?" I prompted. "The feeble and weak? The inferior races?"

Elana pinned him with a sharp gaze. "Child of Darkness, you forget it wasn't always like this. In your lifetime, you will catch only a glimpse of the state of the world. But it helps to understand the bigger picture."

Although Alaric did his best to maintain a casual air, I sensed he was annoyed. "Enlighten us then. What's the bigger picture?"

"There is an imbalance in the world today," she said. "It will not continue. Either we will right ourselves or we will succumb."

"I don't believe in balance," Roger said. "I've always considered dualism to be a primitive belief."

Her eyes widened slightly. "Go on."

"The Slavonic mythology had Bylebog and Chernobog." Roger turned to us. "The White God and the Black God."

"Let me guess," Alaric said. "The White God was daytime and the Black God was nighttime."

"Light and day. Shadows and night," the woman murmured.

"What happens if the world is imbalanced for too long?" I asked.

"There were those who once believed the world would eventually come to an end."

"Are we talking scientists and a well-aimed comet or something else?" Roger asked.

She stuck a finger in her mouth to dislodge a scrap of meat. "Have you never heard of the Twilight of the Gods?"

Alaric laughed. "That's nothing but a fairy tale."

She leveled him with a look. "There are those who would say the same about you."

Roger snickered. "Well, that's you put in your place."

"In that story it was foretold a day would come when giants and monsters would rise from the subterranean regions of the world and overthrow the gods, and the universe would be destroyed."

Alaric splayed his hands. "Well, given that we're all sitting here, I'd say it never came to pass."

Roger tossed a short stick on the fire, creating a satisfying crackling sound. "I don't see any gods around, do you?"

"Life is a cycle, friends," the old woman explained. "What has happened once will happen again. Such is the reason eternity is symbolized by a circle."

Alaric poked the weakening flames with a stick. "If what you say is true, the universe would've been destroyed by now and broken the cycle. You said the world would eventually come to an end, which makes the idea of eternity a myth."

The flames cast an eerie glow on her face as she turned to regard the two vampires. "Perhaps in our story, *you* are the gods."

Everyone fell silent.

Finally Alaric tossed aside the stick and rose to his feet. "I think we've rested long enough. We should go."

I whistled for George. "Thank you for sharing your fire," I told the old woman.

"Take good care and remember," she said, "some roads are best not taken."

We made our way out of the woods and I was relieved to see George ahead of us.

"How much do you want to bet she tells these stories for a living?" Alaric asked. "We got the free version."

"Maybe the story didn't mean the world itself, but the world as we know it," I suggested. "That makes sense if you think about it. The humans who lived before the Great Eruption didn't know supernaturals existed. Gods would've been the obvious choice."

"It isn't worth any further discussion," Alaric said. "It borders on treason."

Somebody was touchy.

We climbed into the minivan. This time when I insisted on driving, Alaric didn't object.

The vampires chatted about Roger's to-do list in Palm Beach while I focused on the road and our surroundings. Finally I pulled into the train station parking lot. It was small with only two working lamp posts, but it would get Roger where he needed to go.

"There's something I've been wanting to mention." Roger said as we exited the minivan. "I heard a ridiculous rumor before I left Palm Beach." He pressed his lips together. "I hate to even repeat it, but I think you need to know what's being said. It could put you at risk during your journey home."

"What is it?" Alaric asked.

"That your father is dead." Roger shook his head in disbelief. "As though anyone could kill King Maxwell."

I shot an alarmed look at Alaric, but I couldn't read his face. This was a problem. If the word was out, we'd have to pick up the pace.

"It's true," Alaric said softly.

I placed a hand on his arm. "Your Highness..."

He shook me off. "You can't tell anyone, Roger. You must swear to it."

Roger gaped at us. "The king is dead?"

Alaric nodded somberly. "Murdered. That's why Britt came for me and that's why I'm headed back to New York. Do you understand now why I need you to hold down the fort? I don't know if or when I'll be back."

Roger stood in stupefied silence for a moment before finally regaining the power of speech. "Who? How?"

"None of that matters," I said. "Go back to Palm Beach and tell no one about the king or about us."

"You never saw us," Alaric emphasized.

Roger pulled the prince into an embrace. "I'm so sorry, friend. All this time you've been grieving and I didn't know."

Alaric patted his friend's back. "It's okay, Roger. You didn't know because I couldn't tell you." He extricated himself from the embrace. "I want you to be safe and that means doing as I tell you."

Roger inhaled deeply, appearing to get his emotions in check. "I will. Just know I'm here for you. I know your relationship with him was complicated, but it still must be difficult for you."

Alaric held up a hand to silence him. "I don't want to talk about that right now. I need to focus on other priorities."

"Understood."

Roger scratched his cheek. "Do you think whoever killed your father will come for you in Palm Beach? I'll need to increase security for the rest of us."

"Take George with you," I said. "He can help."

The pygmy dragon made a noise, but I ignored him.

Roger glanced at the small dragon with trepidation.

"Take him," Alaric insisted. "I'd never forgive myself if anything happened to you because of me."

"George will know how to find me once the threat is over, and if he can't find me for some reason, he knows the way home." I looked at the pygmy dragon. "I'll see you at the apartment if not before then."

George flapped his wings and gave me a hard look with his one good eye. I knew he wasn't happy with the change in plans, but it didn't matter.

If there was one lesson I seemed to learn over and over, it was that we all had to do things we didn't want to do—some of us more often than others.

## SIX

"Where are we?" Alaric asked mid-yawn as he awoke from a nap.

"Not far from Richmond."

He peered at the dashboard. "We need fuel."

"I've got it covered. There's a place I know." Farmville was small, quaint, and surprisingly well-preserved for a town in this region.

"I don't suppose they stock any good whiskey in this place of yours."

"No, but they serve a helluva moonshine. If you don't pee immediately, it'll burn a hole through your bladder."

"Charming."

I drove along Farmville Road. "It's darker than I remember." I was sure there'd been more streetlights, as well as lights from the storefronts.

"Maybe there's an issue with their generator."

We passed beneath the Welcome to Historic Farmville sign and entered the downtown area. I parked in front of an old red brick church and exited the minivan to look around. The town was eerily quiet. Although there were a few cars and trucks parked along the road, the town seemed uninhabited. Nobody was outside. I began peering in windows. The buildings were devoid of people, too.

"This is strange."

Alaric trailed behind me. "How do you know about this place?"

"I stayed here a few times between jobs. The last time was about four-and-a-half years ago. It wasn't abandoned then. Something must've happened."

We walked along the main strip, peering into empty stores and opening the occasional door. A wooden sign was posted on the boarded-up window of an abandoned barbershop. *Beware the Lake* was painted in red.

"I guess we know why the town's been abandoned," Alaric said.

We passed a couple more signs that featured similar warnings.

"Want to check out the lake?" I asked.

He raised an eyebrow. "Aren't you supposed to be keeping me safe from harm? What's your plan—push me in and call it an accident?"

"As tempting as the idea is, no. To be honest, Farmville was a pleasant town in an unpleasant world. I wouldn't mind seeing if there's something I can do about the lake problem."

"Since when did you become a Good Samaritan?"

"It's for entirely selfish reasons. I'd like to come back here someday and have another ice cream sundae at Sweetie's." I still remembered the taste. It had been a decadent decision—ice cream and its accoutrements weren't cheap—but I'd savored every bite and committed the taste to memory.

He smirked. "Do you remember that time with the whipped cream when...?"

I held up a hand. "Stop right there. Not interested."

"You seemed plenty interested at the time."

"Well, times have changed."

"I haven't."

I came to an abrupt stop and looked at him. "Exactly." I returned to the minivan. "We'll refuel first and then swing by the lake."

"How do you know there'll be any fuel left?"

I stepped over an empty paper bag on the sidewalk. "Because it seems like people left in a hurry."

Sure enough, there was plenty of fuel to be had. I filled the tank and drove to the lake.

"Should I wait here?" Alaric asked.

"That's probably best." As I vacated the driver's seat, I heard the sound of the passenger door opening. "What are you doing?"

"You sounded disappointed, so I'm coming with you."

The lake covered about thirty acres. There were well-worn walking trails surrounding it, but most of the trees that once graced the area were long gone.

I suddenly wished George were with us. I could've used a bit of light. One wrong step and I could end up in deep water.

Alaric observed the charcoal lake. "Seems calm to me. Maybe whatever chased everyone away is dead."

A shrill scream pierced the air.

I gave him a pointed look. "You were saying."

He motioned me forward. "You were the one eager to restore the town. You might want to start by saving the screamer."

We followed a trail around the lake. A second scream

told us we were headed in the right direction. When water splashed my clothes, I knew we were close.

"Hang on! I'm coming!" a panicked voice yelled.

My vision adjusted to the scene. A boy—he couldn't have been older than ten—stood at the edge of the lake. Fifteen feet away and partially submerged in water was our monster problem.

"Holy hellfire," I breathed.

Alaric's eyes widened. "Is that a leviathan?"

"I think so."

"I thought they were only found in salt water."

"Apparently they evolved."

The creature had the body of a giant serpent and the head of a dragon, but I'd never known them to inhabit fresh water. It was hard to tell the color of its scales in the darkness, but my money was on green. Its tail was currently coiled around a young girl. The screamer, presumably.

The boy became aware of our presence and pointed. "Please help my sister. Please! I'll give you everything I have."

The pleading note struck a chord in me. Even if I hadn't planned to help, that voice would've swayed me to act.

I faced the leviathan and tried to form a connection. It seemed to sense my presence and turned its head. Two brilliant sunbursts fixed on me.

"That's right," I cooed. "Pay attention to me. I'm the threat."

I concentrated on reaching the blood inside the creature. It felt different from other blood—thicker and more potent. The information shouldn't have been surprising. The leviathan was a relative of the dragon and dragon's blood was sought after for all sorts of supplements and remedies. Wealthy vampires kept vials of it to use for sexual enhancement. Ask me how I know.

I now had the leviathan's full attention. Its head swayed in front of me like a snake in front of a charmer. Its tail dipped into the water, taking the girl with it. If I didn't hurry, she'd drown.

Alaric must've had the same thought because the vampire crept toward the water.

"What are you doing?" I hissed, making sure to keep my hold on the creature's blood.

"Helping. Tell me when you've got full control."

The leviathan resisted my intrusion, but I kept a firm grip. My magic acted as tendrils, slithering around the blood and seizing control of it.

"Now," I said.

The prince dove into the water and swam.

"What's he doing? Is he crazy?" the boy said excitedly.

"He's saving your sister," I said, maintaining my hold on the leviathan. I'd slowed the blood flow so that the creature was too lethargic to move.

"If it falls asleep in the water, will it drown?" the boy asked in a quiet voice.

"It won't fall asleep. It will be unconscious, and the truth is I don't know." It seemed likely sea monsters had a way of staying alive underwater when they were unconscious.

The sound of water splashing suggested that Alaric had retrieved the girl. I couldn't break contact with the leviathan to confirm or I risked losing my hold.

In his haste to help Alaric and his sister, the boy rushed past me and stepped on my foot in the process. It was only a small gesture but enough to break my concentration.

I tried to regain control of the blood, but the leviathan was too strong. "Hurry!"

The leviathan smacked its tail hard on the surface of the water and roared.

"Please don't spit fire," the boy said.

Alaric had the girl on his back and was swimming to shore. The leviathan turned and spotted them.

No. No. No.

I whipped a dagger from my utility belt. "Boy, stand in front of me and bend over. Now!"

To his credit, the boy didn't question the odd request. He *moved*.

I backed up to allow myself a running start. I raced forward and used the boy's back as a springboard. Dagger in hand, I launched myself across the water at the leviathan. I sank the blade into the creature's neck just below its pronounced chin and gripped the handle with both hands. Dragging the dagger in a downward motion, I sliced the creature's throat open and landed in the water.

Blood spilled from the leviathan's body and saturated the water. I swam to safety, still clutching my dagger. I crawled to land as the leviathan groaned. I turned in time to see it slip below the lake's surface.

I remained on my hands and knees for a moment to catch my breath. When I glanced up, I was relieved to see Alaric and the girl in one piece. The girl's brother was drying her off with his own shirt.

"Thank you," the boy said. "You didn't have to do that."

I squeezed the excess water from my hair. "It's okay. I'm glad you're safe."

"I don't think many people would've stopped to save two strangers," the girl said. She was cute as far as kids went. Her light brown hair was styled in two braids and she wore a long-sleeved top that featured the picture of a strawberry in a white bonnet and the words 'berry cute' beneath it.

"I guess you're lucky it was the two of us passing by," I said.

The boy offered his hand. He seemed unsure, as though he'd witnessed the gesture but had never actually done it himself. "I'm Jason and this is my sister, Meredith."

I shook his hand. It felt small and vulnerable in mine. "I'm Britt and this is my friend, Colin."

"How did you end up here?" Alaric asked.

"We stayed the night in one of the houses and then stopped to fish the lake before we set off." Eyes wide, the boy gasped. "Be right back."

He darted to a large rock and retrieved a weathered satchel. He slung the strap over his shoulder and returned to us.

"You didn't see the warning signs about the lake?" I asked. "They were posted on several of the storefronts."

"Can't read," Meredith said. "Never learned."

"We should've left with the others," Jason said, "but Meredith twisted her ankle yesterday and I wanted to give it time to heal."

"Is that your supply bag?" I asked. The satchel looked a little thin and I wagered there wasn't much in there.

The boy seemed flustered. "Sort of."

"Where are you headed?" Alaric asked.

Jason puffed out his birdcage of a chest. "North. We're going to reclaim Washington D.C. Did you know it used to be the capital of the whole country?"

Alaric burst into laughter. "Reclaim it? You do know what it's called now, don't you?"

The boy's eyes remained solemn. "Monster Maze. Wasteland. We know."

"I assume you have a plan," I said.

His head bobbed up and down. "Yep. We're going to swarm the district and make it our own."

Meredith pumped a fist in the air. "Kick those monsters to the curb!"

"I think it might take more than two of you," Alaric said. "There's what—a hundred and twenty pounds between you? And very little of it is muscle."

"We're not alone," Jason said. "We got separated from our group is all."

"We're part of a crusade," Meredith said with the cheery inflection of someone announcing they were finalists in a talent competition.

Alaric raised an eyebrow. "A crusade?"

"Not a religious one," Jason explained. "Our crusade is…" His gaze settled on Alaric and he faltered.

Meredith seemed oblivious to her brother's hesitation. "We're going to overthrow vampires," she chirped.

"Ah, I see. Are we as bad as that?" Alaric sounded vaguely amused.

Meredith realized her faux pas and grabbed her brother's hand for support.

I patted Alaric's shoulder. "Not to worry. This one's on the level. He helped rescue you, remember? Would he do that if he were pure evil?"

"He would if he wants our blood fresh," Jason replied matter-of-factly.

Alaric considered the accusation. "I suppose that's true, but personally I prefer blood that's had a chance to age. Young blood is far too…" He smacked his lips. "Metallic."

The children huddled closer together.

I shot the vampire a look of chastisement. "What my friend means to say is you have nothing to fear from him."

"Well, we're not overthrowing you personally," the boy said. "It's not like you're the king."

"No, he's not the king," I assured them. Not yet anyway.

"Where are your parents?" Alaric asked. "How could they let you travel so far on your own?"

"We don't have any parents," Meredith told us. "The children in the crusade are all orphans."

"Mostly," Jason corrected her. "Some of them left a bad situation."

I knew all about those.

"And you're all human?" I asked.

"Not entirely." Jason crouched down to adjust the tongue of his shoe. "We've got a few werewolves and witches. They're the bossy ones."

"They're going to help us fight the monsters," Meredith declared.

"Yes, they'll be helpful in a fight," I told her. I knew beyond a shadow of a doubt that if I'd encountered this horde of children in my youth, I would've joined them in a heartbeat.

Jason bristled. "We don't need any supers to fight. We've got our own weapons." He clutched the satchel against his chest.

I held out a hand. "May I see? I might be able to offer a few tips."

Alaric tilted his head toward me. "Listen to her. She speaks from experience."

The boy gave me a speculative look. "You fought vampires?"

"Not just fought. Killed," Alaric said.

The children appeared momentarily confused. "But

you're traveling together," Meredith said, her voice rising at the end.

"It's a long story," I told them. "But if you show me what's in the satchel, I might be able to offer some advice."

Keeping his gaze on Alaric as though the vampire might snatch the bag mid-movement, Jason twisted the metal nub and lifted the flap. He produced a wooden box that looked even older than the satchel. The lid was scratched and worn and a piece had broken off a corner. He cradled the box on his forearm and opened it for our inspection.

I peered at the contents. There were three levels, similar to a jewelry box except this box contained an assortment of seemingly unrelated objects. The top level housed three religious crosses and four vials of different-colored liquids. The second level included a revolver, a silver blade so old it had turned green, an atomizer, and a book. The base level helped the rest of the items make sense. Nestled inside were three stakes, a wooden mallet, and a corked bottle that I assumed contained holy water.

Alaric whistled. "An antique vampire killing kit. Where'd you find a gem like that?"

"My grandpa gave it to me before he died," Jason said. "Said it's been in our family for generations, since before the Eternal Night. Told me to take good care of it because I might need it someday."

"And you decided to need it sooner than someday," I surmised.

Alaric tapped each of the three crosses in the kit. "Allow me to lighten your load. These are useless. Old wives' tales."

Meredith's mouth formed a tiny 'o.'

Her brother's eyebrows knitted together. "Really? They don't do nothin'?"

"Afraid not. Watch, I'll show you." The vampire

removed the largest of the three crosses and pressed it against his cheek. "No impact."

Jason's mouth turned down at the corners. "Well, that's disappointing."

"What about the holy water?" Meredith asked.

"Another myth," Alaric told her. "Would you like me to demonstrate?"

Jason shook his head. "We might need those drops of water for drinkin'. Wouldn't be right to waste them."

"Good thinking," I said. They weren't stupid. That would get them farther than most kids, but still didn't guarantee their safety.

"I suppose your crusading friends are armed with crosses and holy water," Alaric remarked.

The children nodded in unison.

"There are a few ways to kill a vampire," I said. "Would you like to hear them?"

Alaric shot me an aggrieved look. "If you must."

I wiggled my fingers. "You can go over by that tree stump out of earshot."

"I'm a vampire. I have to go farther than that if you expect me not to hear anything."

"Don't you already know the ways you can be killed?" Meredith asked.

A smile tugged at the prince's lips. "You're right. I'll listen and offer confirmation."

I counted on my fingers. "Decapitation. Stake through the heart. Electrocution. Basically the same as killing any other species except it requires more effort because they're strong, fast, and quick healers. Unlike the rest of us, though, they're susceptible to sunlight. Too much and poof! Ashes to ashes. Dust to dust." I glanced at the prince. "Does that cover it?"

"You didn't tell them how *you* kill us."

"Because it doesn't matter. They can't do it."

Jason jumped on the idea. "What is it? What can you do? Is it what you tried to do to that monster?"

"It's nothing you'd be able to replicate. Stick to the skills you can master." I took one of the vials from the box. "Do you know what's in these?"

"No. Grandpa didn't know either. He just knew about the holy water."

I unscrewed the lid and sniffed. The liquid smelled faintly of rosewater. "You could use this to wash your face, but that's about it."

Alaric removed the revolver and inspected it. "This won't do any good either."

"Not against you, but might help against thieves or monsters," Jason said.

"It's more likely to kill you than them." He placed it back in the box. "But I won't deprive you of your defensive measures."

"Keep the mallet. It might come in handy as a tool if you intend to rebuild an entire city," I told them.

"We have other tools with us," Jason said. "At least the group does."

"Do you know the route these crusaders of yours are taking?" Alaric asked.

Jason nodded. "We can catch up. Their plan is to approach from the west. They don't move very fast with all those kids."

His mouth twitched. "No, I suppose not."

"More like a giant sloth," Meredith added. Her eyes popped. "Do you think there might be giant sloths in the Wasteland?"

"Not that I've heard. Kids, would you excuse us for a minute?" I offered them a reassuring smile.

Meredith rolled her eyes. "We know. The grown-ups need to have a conversation."

I tugged Alaric out of earshot. "We need to escort these kids to the Wasteland."

"Escort them? You're meant to be escorting me."

"Can't I do both? The district is on the way."

Alaric barked a laugh. "You say that like we're stopping for coffee. We're not going through D.C. We specifically agreed to go around to avoid death or dismemberment."

"I know, but we can't let an entire generation of children walk to their doom. We have to get there ahead of them and clear the path. If the kids are arriving from the west, we can approach from the south and get there ahead of them."

Alaric gaped at me. "You, me, and what army? We're supposed to be sneaking back to New York in secrecy and now you want to announce our presence to every monster in the Wasteland?"

"I'm not proposing we send trumpets and a red carpet in first."

The vampire drew a deep breath. "As impressive as we are—and let's be honest, we are impressive—you and I can't do it alone."

Relief rushed through me. He was actually considering it. I thought for sure he'd offer a firm no and be done with it.

"Then we'll enlist reinforcements," I suggested.

"How? We'd have to give away our location. That would put us in jeopardy for the rest of the journey."

"Once we're there, New York isn't far. We have to try."

Alaric studied my face. "You see yourself in them."

"I see all of humanity in them," I shot back. But he was

right. I also saw a seven-year-old witch who'd been abandoned by every adult in her life and forced to fend for herself.

"And I suppose you'll want to take Jason and Meredith with us?"

I nodded. "At least I'll know they're safe."

Alaric paced in front of me, debating. Finally he said, "Roger will help. I'll send word to him."

"He'll never make it in time."

"He's not hiding from anyone. He and George can travel by train."

I nodded. "I'll get a message to Liam."

"Who's Liam?" I detected a note of jealousy in his tone, which surprised me.

"My neighbor. You've met him. He works as an engineer for your family. We can trust him."

The prince dragged a hand through his hair. "We have no idea what we're up against."

"You're right. It's probably suicide."

Alaric's gaze met mine. A burst of energy sparked inside me as our eyes locked. "You've got that determined look I remember so well. Very sexy."

My pulse quickened and I couldn't tear my gaze from him.

"This is the part where you say 'now isn't the time, Alaric.'"

I licked my lips. "How do I send a message?"

His gaze met mine. "I think you already did."

My cheeks grew warm and I looked away. "I'm talking about sending a message to Roger. I need a number for him that won't be intercepted by anyone else."

"Oh. Right. We have a private line. I can give you the number."

"I figured as much."

I'd need to find a place with good cellular service. No small feat in this area.

We returned to the siblings who seemed to be in the midst of a disagreement. I delivered the good news, but they still seemed distracted.

"What's going on?" I asked.

Meredith nudged her brother. "Tell them."

Jason stared at the ground.

"Tell us what?" Alaric prompted.

Meredith reached into Jason's back pocket. "I knew you looked familiar. This was in our bag." She handed over a folded sheet of paper. Jason tried to snatch it away, but Alaric grabbed it first. Vampire reflexes were a bitch.

The prince unfolded the paper and frowned. "Hmm. This complicates matters."

Meredith glared at her brother. "See? I told you."

I peered over Alaric's shoulder. On the paper was written *Wanted Alive: Answers to Britt. Dangerous Witch.* My image and a phone number were sketched underneath.

"Found it stuck to a pole in town," Jason admitted.

"We took it so we could play Tic-tac-toe," Meredith added.

"Who would've done this?" I asked. We were in House August territory. Only the queen would've been able to authorize this. It made no sense.

"At least they want you alive," Meredith said. "That's good, right?"

"I thought I'd be able to tell who issued the order based on the contact information, but I don't recognize the number," Alaric said. "Maybe we should call."

I gaped at him. "And what? Report a sighting of me? Does that sound smart to you?"

"I can say I think I saw you in Athens. Somewhere far from here."

"And what if they didn't drop flyers in Athens? What if they know you're lying? Then they'll be alerted to the fact that I've been somewhere they left their calling card." I shook my head. "Best not to contact them."

"What'd you do?" Jason asked.

"A lot of things, but none of them are relevant now." I plucked the flyer from Alaric's hand and stuffed it in my pocket. The prince was right—this turn of events complicated matters. "Excuse us another minute." I dragged the prince out of earshot.

"Do you think someone knows my mother sent you to find me? That's their way of flushing us out?"

"It's possible, but I doubt it. She was adamant about telling no one." I glanced at the children. They'd been through enough. I couldn't endanger them with our baggage. "We need to split up. At least until we're out of this area. You take the kids and I'll meet you at the southern border of the Wasteland."

Alaric blanched. "Why should I take the kids?"

"Because people will be looking for me, not you, and if there *are* assassins searching for Prince Alaric, they won't be looking for a vampire with two human children."

"Which way will you go?"

I hesitated. "I think it's best if I don't tell you—for your own safety."

Alaric groaned. "What about the minivan?"

"You take it. You've got the kids. I'll find another way." I removed the Monster Masher from the holster and handed it to him. "The ammo's in the bag in the minivan."

Alaric stared at the gun in his hand. "I don't like this."

"You don't have to like it. You just have to make it to the rendezvous point."

He shook his head. "I should never have agreed to this. I should've made us stick to the plan."

We couldn't back out now. There were two kids relying on us and I refused to let them down.

I strengthened my resolve. "I'll see you at the southern entrance. Take care of yourself, Alaric."

He offered a sad smile. "So you can gain your freedom? That's what my mother offered you in exchange for my safe return, isn't it?"

I looked directly into those green eyes I knew so well. The ones that shared the same gold flecks as his mother's. He really was the perfect specimen. Beautiful on the outside. *And a monster on the inside*, I reminded myself.

"Of course," I told him without a trace of regret. "Why else would I be here?"

# SEVEN

I managed to find an abandoned bicycle in Farmville and rode it approximately thirty miles northeast to the next inhabited town. The downside of no vehicle was that I needed to refuel my body far more often and for far longer than the minivan.

The town of Cartersville was nestled alongside the James River, which I needed to cross. Whatever bridges that once existed were long gone, so it was take your chances swimming, whittle your kayak, or pay for a boat ride. I'd figure out my options over a plate of hot food and a much-needed drink.

Due to the late hour, most of the establishments were closed. Cartersville was a different atmosphere from New York. Even after all this time, the latter was known as the City That Never Sleeps. Round-the-clock darkness made that title even easier to earn. Apparently old habits die hard in Cartersville and the business owners stuck to more traditional hours.

I parked the bike in front of the only place that appeared open. The bar looked a little down on its luck and

I had to imagine everybody on the inside matched the outside. Whatever. I was grabbing a bite to eat, not moving in.

I entered the bar as discreetly as possible to get the lay of the land. A dozen patrons were scattered throughout the room. No vampires that I could see. A handful of humans. A werewolf couple groped each other by the restroom. Why they didn't slip inside and save the rest of us from their PDA, I had no idea. Too drunk, most likely.

I crossed the room to the bar and settled on a stool away from the other patrons. The portly bartender gave me a curious look. No doubt he could tell I was from out of town. He probably knew the personal details of everybody else in the place. Town watering holes were hotbeds of gossip and insider knowledge.

I ordered the root vegetable and rice platter and the tallest glass of water possible.

"No beer?" the bartender asked. "We just got a new shipment of moonshine, too. Local flavor. Real spicy."

"No, thanks. I just rode a bike thirty miles. I need to hydrate."

He got the glass of water first and then walked away to place the food order. I gulped down the water and waited for a refill. In the meantime, I scoped out the interior. There was a wooden board with announcements tacked to it and I recognized the sketch of me on one of them. Thankfully it was partially hidden by another paper requesting contributors for a new blood bank in Richmond. The pay was decent. I bet half these patrons had contributed blood at one time or another. Sometimes it was the easiest and fastest way for humans to pay bills.

The bartender set both a fresh glass of water and a hot plate of food in front of me. I took a second to inspect the vegetables. Once in a while some scammer would try to serve celery stalks on a bed of rice and call it a vegetable platter.

Stomach growling, I picked up my fork. This was the real deal.

"Anything else?" the bartender asked.

"I'm looking to cross the river after this. Any suggestions?"

He nodded. "Junior can take you."

I craned my neck to observe the other patrons. "Junior's not one of these guys with his head in a pitcher of beer, I hope."

The bartender snorted. "Nope. He rents a room above the bar. Works the late shift."

"Tell him he has a paying customer." I tapped my plate. "As soon as I finish up here. The green beans are perfect, by the way."

He beamed with pride. "It's my personal mission to make sure they're not too soggy. One of my pet peeves growing up. Soggy vegetables."

"Hats off to you, sir. Achievement unlocked." A sharp cry from behind the wall interrupted our pleasant exchange. The bartender flinched at the sound but didn't otherwise move. "What's in that back room?" Junior was upstairs, not in an adjacent room, so that ruled him out.

The bartender gave a quick shake of his head. It was more than a simple refusal to answer. Sweat beaded his brow and his eyes radiated fear. Whatever was back there, he didn't want to acknowledge it out loud.

Well, now I had to know.

Downing my second water, I slid off the stool and sauntered toward the closed door. I felt the bartender's eyes following me and wondered whether he'd intervene or alert whomever was on the other side of the wall.

He did neither.

My fingers curled around the handle and I gently turned the knob. It opened with a soft click. I slipped inside and closed the door behind me.

The room was bathed in darkness except for anemic light that emanated from a single candle. It took a moment for my eyes to adjust. A vampire in a charcoal-colored suit and a black shirt stood at a table. Across from him was a woman seated in a chunky metal chair. A book lay open on the table between them.

The vampire glanced at me, nostrils flaring. "Do you mind? As you can see, we're in the middle of a meeting."

"I heard a cry and thought someone might be hurt."

The woman was breathing heavily and I realized her wrists were bound to the chair. Some meeting.

I could dispatch one scumbag vampire off the record. Nobody here would tell, certainly not his victim.

The vampire smiled, showing a set of dainty fangs. The points were small and elegant. Form over function.

I showed no sign of leaving.

The vampire blew out an annoyed breath. "When I said we're in the middle of a meeting, that wasn't meant as an invitation to join us."

"Oh, no? You look like the kind of guy who might enjoy two women at the same time. I'm in an adventurous mood, so I thought I'd test the waters."

I moved closer to the table for a better view of the book.

The vampire removed his suit jacket and placed it on the back of the empty chair beside him. He dusted off the shoulders with precise movements and adjusted the material so that the seams formed a straight line across the back.

Once he was satisfied with the placement of the jacket, he returned his attention to me.

"My name is Vincent Dufresne. This is my new friend, Emily. And you are?"

"Britt." I waited for a flash of recognition. Britt the Bloody. Britt the Blood Witch. Britt the Nightcrawler. I had a dozen names and most of them included my real one—except one.

"Death Bringer?" I tacked on and waited.

Vincent didn't flinch. "I'm speaking to my new friend about certain activities she engages in. A boy in the nearby town reported that a woman named Emily gave him a balm that promised to heal his mother's wounds."

"I already told you there's nothing magic about the balm. It's science." Her voice was a hoarse whisper.

His eyes turned to slits. "I know magic when I see it."

"Like porn?" I offered.

Vincent was not amused. "Do you know who I am?"

"Vincent Dufresne. We covered that part, remember?"

His mouth tightened. "And do you know what I do?"

"I'm going to go out on a limb and say torture women with monologues."

His jaw clicked closed. "I am the Inquisitor."

My throat ran dry. An actual inquisitor. Not just an inquisitor. *The* Inquisitor.

Well, shit.

I'd heard countless stories about him, beginning when I was a little girl in Lancaster. The coven was terrified of the Inquisitor. He traveled the realm on behalf of the Houses, rooting out magic users, particularly those who posed a threat to vampire rule.

"You wrote the book," I said. He literally wrote the

manual that other inquisitors used to interrogate magical suspects. I cut a glance at the table. "Is that it?"

Vincent placed a proprietary hand on the open book. "If you mean the manual, then yes. This book serves as a guide on the best methods for eliciting an honest response from your subject."

"Subject...or victim?"

"Decide for yourself." He returned his attention to Emily. "Who taught you magic?"

"No one. I don't do magic, sir. I told you already, it's science."

Vincent was undeterred. "What do you do as part of your practice? Read entrails? Necromancy?"

I groaned. "Does sweet Emily look like she's a necromancer? Get a grip, Vincent." I plucked a dagger from my belt and approached the table. "You're interrogating this woman on the word of a little boy?"

"I'm permitted to take action even under the mere whisper of a rumor."

"I know what you're permitted to do. You're permitted to encourage people to turn over their friends and neighbors. The proceedings are done in secret with no right to appeal. Is there a tribunal in town or do you plan to act as judge, jury, and executioner all by yourself?" I clucked my tongue. "And people say men can't multitask."

Cold fury radiated from Vincent. "What's your last name, Britt?"

Ignoring him, I sliced through Emily's ropes with the dagger. "Go. Find a safe place to stay until this blowhard leaves town."

Emily didn't need to be told twice. She raced from the room, practically tripping over her own feet in an effort to get away.

Vincent regarded me coolly. "What type of magic do you practice? Don't deny it. I can smell it on you like a cancer."

"You can smell cancer? In that case, you should consider a career change. I hear cancer detection is in high demand in certain circles." Prior to the Great Eruption, there'd been great strides in cancer research, but much of that knowledge was lost to us now.

"Did you refer to yourself as a Blood Witch? Did I hear that correctly?"

"Your ears still work. Congratulations." I still held the dagger in my hand, which didn't escape the vampire's notice. His gaze rested on the blade and stayed there for a beat too long.

"And what is it you can do? Make others bleed? Because I have news for you, we can all do that."

He was trying to goad me into revealing the specifics of my power. Fat chance.

"Before you do something you'll regret, you should know I have special dispensation to use magic."

Vincent closed the book with a thud. "Is that so? From whom?"

"House August." I couldn't tell him the reason I was here, of course, but I could at least dissuade him from trying to judge and execute me in one fell swoop. I had a feeling the vampire derived a little too much pleasure from his work.

"And I assume you can provide documentation of this special dispensation?"

"Not today, but run my name past the Powers-That-Be and they'll tell you. Talk to Olis, the Director of Security."

He chuckled. "Oh, most certainly. And by the time I've

discovered your lie, you'll be long gone. Do I look like a fool to you?"

"A black shirt with a charcoal jacket?" I held my index finger and thumb close together. "Maybe this much."

His eyes blazed with indignation. Vincent the Inquisitor was sensitive about his fashion sense. Got it.

He took a purposeful step toward me and I focused on his blood in an effort to form a connection. I was met with—nothing. His insides felt like a hollow chamber, as though there was no blood at all. What on earth?

Then I saw the charm around his neck. The color of the black opal blended with the fabric of his shirt. No wonder he wore black. He didn't want his hypocrisy to be obvious.

"So it's okay for you to benefit from magic, but not a boy trying to heal his mother? Did you even pay for that charm or did you torture the magic out of one of your victims?"

He sniffed. "I encounter magic users on a regular basis. I must have the means to defend myself against their dark arts."

I had to give the vampire credit—Vincent was resourceful. He managed to block my all-access pass to his blood with that defensive charm that acted as a ward. Of course he didn't realize I had the means to bypass his personal security system. Still holding my dagger, I flicked the blade across my palm and then tossed the dagger at him.

The ward shattered and I quickly attached my magic to his blood. His eyes rounded as he felt my presence.

"No! Whatever you're doing, I demand that you stop at once."

"Or what?" I focused on the pulsing blood in his veins and slowed the flow. Not enough to kill him but enough to teach him a lesson. He stumbled to the side and pressed a hand flat on the table to steady himself.

"There's something you should know about me, witch," he rasped.

"You're a misogynist? Already figured that one out."

The vampire managed a smile. "I have prepared for every eventuality when it comes to witches."

Like I said—resourceful.

He dipped a hand into his trouser pocket and withdrew a small object. Before I could get a good look, he tossed it at me.

Purple dust exploded around me and I felt my magic snap back. Whatever the substance was, it broke my connection to the vampire's blood.

I was still coughing when he attacked.

Vincent was too fancy to use his elegant fangs, though. The vampire retrieved a concealed a dagger of his own. I turned to the side as he slid the blade into my flesh. Pain jolted me and it felt like all the air left my lungs.

I pressed my hand against the wound and was relieved to realize it was only a flesh wound. Didn't stop the pain, but at least it wasn't a fatal strike.

"Is that the best you can do, fancy pants?"

Vincent raised the dagger, ready to throw, when a figure bounded into the room on all fours. The reddish-brown wolf lunged at the vampire's side and knocked him to the floor. Snarling jaws morphed into the soft features of a woman's face but the fur-covered body remained the same. I'd never seen anything like it.

"You may have boned up on witches, but looks like you failed to prepare for werewolves," the she-wolf told Vincent. Human limbs replaced four legs, but they were still covered in the same reddish-brown fur. "You know what they say— fail to prepare and prepare to fail."

I heard the crunch of bone as she twisted his arm

behind him, eliciting a sharp cry of pain from the vampire. "Do you know who I am?" he asked between ragged breaths.

"I don't care who you are. You're to leave this one alone, got it?" She released him and stood upright in her unusual form.

I had questions.

Clutching his injured arm, the Inquisitor staggered to his feet. "My authority extends beyond magic users. You will pay for your interference in House matters."

The werewolf's hands cemented to her furry hips. "You don't work for any House."

"You're right. I don't," he said, his lips curving into a cruel smile. "I work for all of them."

The werewolf didn't seem to care. She kneed him in the crotch with enough force to topple the Empire State Building. The vampire whimpered and slid to the floor.

"Alfred, time to take out the trash," she called over her shoulder.

The bartender entered the room. He took one look at the pile of vampire on the floor and choked.

"You said you wouldn't do anything crazy," Alfred accused.

The werewolf waved a hand. "How is this crazy? Crazy would've been stringing him up in the town square to make an example out of him. Or slicing off his head and mounting it over by the highway exit." She motioned to the vampire in a ta-da gesture. "This is restraint at its finest."

Alfred hurried across the room to the vampire. "I am so sorry, Mr. Dufresne. I thought she was coming in for the witch. If I had realized what would happen, I would've stopped her. Please don't revoke my license. This place is my livelihood." He helped the Inquisitor to his feet and escorted him from the room.

"My book," Vincent croaked.

"And his jacket," I said. Swiping the charcoal jacket from the back of the chair, I settled it across the bartender's shoulders.

"Thank you," I told the werewolf, once the men were gone.

"Don't thank me yet. Alfred was right. I didn't come in here for the vampire. I came in here for you."

Well, that news was unexpected.

She folded her furry arms. "You are one dangerous witch, although I've met scarier ones than you. I once met a witch who could shoot lightning from her fingertips." Her lips formed a vague smile. "I watched her light up an entire canyon just by glowing. Can you believe that?"

A strange comfort washed over me, knowing there were more witches like me. Different. That I wasn't as alone in this world as I believed.

"How can you do this?" I motioned to her half-wolf appearance.

"Granny was a witch. My siblings and cousins are all regular werewolves. I got the weird gene."

"Aren't you worried about the Inquisitor?"

"I'm more worried about you. I've been waiting on you for a long time, girl," she drawled.

"To hire me?"

She cackled. "No, silly. To kill you."

"Why did you save me from the Inquisitor if you want me dead?"

"Because it's not proper revenge if I don't do it myself. I want the satisfaction of being the one to escort you from this world."

"If you escort me, you come with me. That means you die, too."

She snorted. "Worth it."

"How did you know where to find me?" I was only passing through and it was mere coincidence that I decided to investigate the cry of pain in the back room of the bar.

"Didn't you notice the flyers about you? There's a bounty in the small print. Somebody in the bar recognized you and called me."

Now it made sense. These flyers weren't new, handed down by the queen or anyone else in House August. I thought it was unlikely the queen had issued the order and now I knew for sure.

"I made that flyer four-and-a-half years ago," the werewolf admitted. "I lived in hope that one day you'd come back to these parts and I'd get my revenge."

Part of me was relieved to know the flyer's origin wasn't House August, although it meant we'd separated for nothing. And now I was here by myself, fighting an Inquisitor *and* a vengeful werewolf. Yippee.

"You know my name. Why don't you tell me yours?"

"Meghan Dunne."

"Tell me, Meghan. What did I do to you that requires revenge? I don't deal in shifters. Never have."

"Doesn't mean shifters aren't collateral damage for you." She pressed her lips together. "Remember a vampire named Ben Boreas?"

I filed through my mental catalogue of hits. "He lived not far from here." It had been a fast job. Didn't pay much, but I'd accepted because I was in the area and the depiction of the vampire I'd been given wasn't flattering. The vampires that hired me described him as depraved and beyond help.

"That's right. As a matter of fact, he lived with me not far from here. I'd been away at the time, traveling for work. Imagine coming home to discover your true love is already dead and buried." Her eyes brimmed with unshed tears. "Didn't even get to say goodbye."

"Technically, they don't bury vampires…"

She glared at me. "It's just an expression, okay? The point is he was gone and you're the one who did it. And now you're going to pay."

Snarling, the werewolf lunged.

I grabbed her wrists to keep her claws from slicing me.

"You're pretty strong," I said through gritted teeth. It wasn't often I got to fight a werewolf unless you counted Liam after a long night of drinking.

"It's the partial form," she said with great effort. "Being able to use my human arms while still half wolf is a huge advantage." She wiggled her hands. "Opposable thumbs."

During the fleeting moment her thumbs were lifted, I managed to sweep a foot behind her leg and push her backward. She fell flat on her back. I straddled her and pinned her arms to the floor.

"They told me he preyed on children."

"They lied," she growled. "Don't you do your own research?"

"Not really."

"Maybe you ought to start."

She obviously didn't know what had become of me, not that she'd care. Servitude was probably too good for me in her eyes.

"His family disowned him when he married me. They would've said anything to ruin his good name. They hated that he chose me over them. Imagine if they knew about Granny. They probably would've tried to kill me, too."

My head began to spin. They'd taken out a hit on their own son because he'd chosen to marry a werewolf?

They'd done more than cast him out for being different. They'd murdered him.

*I'd* murdered him.

I released my grip on the werewolf and she took the opportunity to clock me in the face. I reeled backward as blood spilled from my nose.

"Where are they?" she growled.

"Where's who?"

"His father. The one who hired you."

"I have no idea. It was years ago." And a lot had happened between then and now.

"They fled after Ben died. They knew I'd come after them and they were right, but the trail went cold."

I pinched the bridge of my nose to stop the flow of blood. "I don't know where they are. I don't keep former clients as pen pals."

"His father is David Boreas. He was a bigwig in this area. Not a lesser royal, but he had connections. I think House August set them up somewhere else in the territory and I want to know where."

"I might be able to find out for you, but not if I'm dead."

Fur sprouted on her face. If she fully transformed, there'd be no reasoning with her. One of us would end up killing the other and the cycle would continue. My pulse sped up. I had to get through to her *right now*.

"Meghan, stop! I'm sorry for what I did. If I could take it back, I would. I swear."

Her head tilted as though she wasn't sure she'd heard me correctly. "You're sorry? You think that's going to make it better?"

Her brow enlarged and more fur appeared on her cheeks.

"Of course not, but you still deserve to hear that." I splayed my hands to keep her at bay. "I understand why you want to hurt me, but I don't want to hurt you."

"I don't want to hurt you either. I want to kill you." She tried to force my arms down. "I don't even care if you suffer, as long as you die."

My past had caught up with me in spectacular fashion. I'd spent the majority of the journey feeling bitter about my romantic past with Alaric, how much pain he'd caused me. And here I considered myself the walking wounded.

Meghan's pain was so much worse.

Her head came down so hard on my forehead that my teeth rattled. I was sure my skull was about to split in two. The pain momentarily blinded me. If I didn't do something quickly, Meghan would make good on her promise to kill me. Even if I deserved it, I couldn't let that happen. I had my own promises to keep.

Her mouth started to elongate. If she turned full wolf, it was game over.

She left me no choice. I had to stop her now. I concentrated on her chest and the blood that flowed in and out of her heart. My magic snapped into place as a connection formed. I acted a little too swiftly but only because I had to stop her shifting.

The werewolf clutched her chest. "Do it," she rasped. She collapsed in a heap.

I rolled to my feet. She stared up at me, mouth agape but unable to speak.

"Like I said, I don't want to hurt you. I'm sorry for what I did to your husband. To Ben. I'd like to tell you I'm not that witch anymore, but to some extent, I still am." I backed away from her. "But not today, Meghan Dunne. Not today."

I released my hold on her heart. She rolled on to her stomach and gasped for air, clawing at the floor. Then she vomited.

Once I was sure she was stable, I turned and walked away.

Junior was waiting for me outside the bar. I paid the man and he ferried me and one rusty bicycle across the James River.

I thought about Meghan and Ben with every pump of my legs on the pedals. I hated the witches of my coven for blindly following the orders of the elders, but I'd done exactly the same. I'd accepted jobs without questions and I hadn't simply exiled my targets.

I'd murdered them.

Part of me justified my actions by remembering they were vampires. Our oppressors. And it was vampires that hired me to kill their own kind. The rest of the world would thank me for my service. But the look in Meghan's eyes told a different story. Then my thoughts turned to Prince Alaric.

No. I refused to fall down that emotional rabbit hole.

I kept pedaling, fueled by shame. I had so much to atone for. The coven had hurt me and I'd shaped that pain into a weapon and wielded it against everyone in my path. I had to do better.

My legs turned to jelly and my back ached. I was accustomed to physical exercise but not on a bicycle. I was beginning to think I wouldn't make it when I passed through Fredericksburg.

Almost there.

When I finally climbed off the bicycle, I nearly wept

from relief. I rubbed my aching butt cheeks. Talk about saddle sore.

"Would it have killed me to designate a specific meeting place?" I mumbled to myself. A gas station. A diner. Anything other than a vague reference to the "southern border of the Wasteland." All these complicated feelings I'd been experiencing had clouded my judgment.

I scanned the horizon. Up ahead was the Potomac River. There was no way they would've crossed without me. Beyond the river was the dreaded Monster Maze. Nobody came out of there alive. Maybe it would serve me right to die there. At least it would be for a noble cause.

For once.

A lone figure appeared on the horizon and I flexed my fingers, prepared to reach for my daggers. Then I saw a second figure—this one flying directly above the other's head and my spirits soared. I'd know that shape anywhere.

"George," I cried.

The cavalry had arrived.

# EIGHT

"What took you so long?" the prince demanded the moment I was within earshot. "You're the last to arrive."

"Nice to see you, too. Hit a few bumps in the road."

"You mean you hit a few people and gave them bumps?" Jason asked.

I ruffled the boy's hair. "Something like that. How's the minivan?"

"Made it here in one piece," the prince replied. "Fixed a flat tire in Williamsburg."

"Colin has awful taste in music," Meredith added.

Alaric shot her an aggrieved look. "Hey, we could barely get any reception. Most of what you heard was static."

"Better than your 'music.'" She used air quotes around the word.

"I hope Roger's been treating you well," I said to the pygmy dragon. He didn't snarl or scowl, so I chalked it up to a win.

"I thought you wanted to stick to the shadows and survive," Roger said. "This idea seems more like a death wish to me."

"It wasn't the original plan," Alaric admitted, "but sometimes plans change."

"Have you been introduced to Jason and Meredith?" I gestured to the children.

Roger's eyebrows inched up. "Man, you two were busy while I was gone. How many years has it been?"

Alaric told his friend about the crusade.

Roger whistled. "Has anyone told the kids that sounds insane?"

A Liam-shaped shadow appeared on the horizon.

"Ha! I'm not the last to arrive," I said, jabbing a finger in the direction of the werewolf.

"Of all the places to meet up, you sure chose the worst one," Liam lamented as he approached us. "I had to take the long way, too. Otherwise we would've been at opposite ends of the Wasteland."

I hugged him. "I'm so glad you came. Did you bring what I asked?"

The werewolf slipped the strap of his backpack off his shoulder. "Everything's in here. Don't shake it or we might lose the battle before it's begun."

"How did you get bamboozled into this?" Roger asked.

"Because she asked me," the werewolf said. "I'd do anything for Britt."

"Apparently so would I," the prince replied. "Otherwise we wouldn't be here."

I stopped the warmth in its tracks before it could spread through my body. No way was I letting His Royal Jackass give me the warm fuzzies. This body was officially fuzzy-free.

Roger leaned closer to the prince. "May I have a word with the two of you, please?"

The three of us peeled away from the group.

"Before we charge in there, you should know the word is spreading about your father."

Fear and anger blazed in Alaric's eyes. "How?"

"I don't know, but it's reached Palm Beach. I've intercepted a handful of inquiries. Everybody wants to know where you are."

The prince appeared to collect himself. "We knew it would happen eventually. We just hoped to buy ourselves time."

"There's more, I'm afraid." Roger hesitated. "House Nilsson is to blame."

Alaric flinched. "They've claimed responsibility?"

"No, but your mother says she has evidence."

"What kind of evidence?" I pressed.

"She didn't say."

"You spoke to her directly?" I asked.

Roger nodded. "I called the compound once it was clear the story was out. She sounded distraught to say the least. I told her you were making progress and that seemed to calm her, but she intends to assemble the troops and move against them."

Alaric clenched his hands into fists. "Before I get back?"

"That's how it sounded. She doesn't know what to do and is probably listening to every conflicting piece of advice."

Alaric covered his face with his hand. "This is bad."

"Nobody wants war, Your Highness," he said.

"Well, somebody does," I countered. "Otherwise, they wouldn't have assassinated the most powerful king in the land." I glanced at the Wasteland. "Maybe we should shift gears."

"No." The prince's response was so firm and swift that it took me off guard. "I told these children I would help them. What kind of prince would I be if I went back on my word?"

"We have no idea what we'll be facing in there," I said.

"And we didn't know when we agreed either. Nothing's changed."

I felt torn. I had a duty to House August to protect the prince at all costs. To bring him home safely and gain my freedom.

But what good was my freedom if I'd spend the rest of my life haunted by the faces of children I chose not to save?

"I think we're biting off more than we can chew," I said weakly. The Potomac River was now all that stood between us and the former nation's capital.

Alaric pivoted to face the desolate expanse. "How do you eat an elephant?"

Roger cringed. "We tried that once, remember? It didn't go as planned."

"I don't mean that." Alaric looked at me. "One bite at a time, right?"

I nodded. "Except I'd like to dissuade you from trying to eat elephant again. They're incredibly intelligent animals with a strong sense of community."

"It was a drunken dare," he objected. "I doubt we would've gone through with it."

"Why do grown-ups do stupid things when they drink?" Meredith asked.

Nobody had noticed her standing just outside our little circle.

Alaric glared at her. "Listen, Half Pint. Nobody asked you."

"Are you really a prince?" she asked.

There didn't seem to be a reason to conceal the truth

anymore. Nobody in this group would be alerting the enemy.

Alaric stooped to answer her. "I am. Prince Alaric of House August."

Her brow furrowed. "I like you."

"And why is that a problem?"

"Because one day we're going to kick you to the curb."

Alaric patted her bony shoulder. "But that day is not today, is it? In the meantime, I would be honored to fight alongside you."

Meredith's eyes shone with relief.

"Is this it?" Liam interrupted, making a sweeping gesture with his arm. "This is the whole attack squadron?"

"Afraid so," I told him. "We're working on short notice and trying to prevent a massacre."

"I don't think this counts as a massacre," Liam replied.

I lowered my voice. "That's because the other two hundred children haven't arrived yet."

The werewolf balked. "Are you serious?"

"What about the phrase 'children's crusade' did you not understand?"

"You rushed to get here ahead of them and take on the monsters." Liam gave me an appraising look. "What's gotten into you? You're usually the one killing people, not saving them."

"I would never hurt a child."

Liam wagged a finger at me. "Not unless it was a glamour. Remember that witch you told me about..."

I shook my head. "There are children present, Liam."

"Right. Inappropriate."

I turned to survey the gunmetal-grey landscape. The Wasteland wasn't an exaggeration. Even from this vantage point, I could see that most of the buildings had been razed but the debris remained. Thanks to the different shapes and textures of the debris, the faint outline of a maze was visible. No sign of monsters though.

Yet.

"It wasn't always like this." I heard the wise woman's words tumble from my lips. "Life is a cycle, although it's less obvious to us than it was to those who came before us."

"Because of the sun?" Jason asked.

I nodded. "There was more balance then. Light and darkness. Life and death. Seasons. You would watch plants die but know they would grow again without intervention. It was nature."

Liam scanned the horizon. "This place is everything I dreamed of and more."

"You have weird dreams," the prince commented.

"No, I mean I've always wanted to fight real monsters. The closest I ever came was shouting at some guy for letting the door close in my face. I mean, really. How hard is it to hold the door open for someone behind you? It's the collapse of civilization."

Alaric cut a glance at me. "Is he always like this?"

"Oh, yeah. One hundred percent," Liam said, answering for me.

"Good," the prince said. "We're going to need all the crazy we can get."

Liam grinned broadly. "Now you're speaking my language. When do we start?"

Crossing the river was the first hurdle. It served as a natural boundary from the rest of civilization so no one was eager to build a bridge or provide transport like they might do for other bodies of water.

To my right, a splotch of white in the murk snagged my

attention. Unbelievable. A single white flower floated on the surface.

"Is that a lotus?" Roger asked.

It couldn't be. Flowers couldn't possibly grow in the Wasteland. There was no magic here.

I didn't expect Meredith to dart forward. The little girl was fast—and apparently hadn't learned her lesson from the leviathan.

"Meredith, stop!" I yelled.

She dropped to her knees and reached for the flower. As she pulled the lotus toward her, it became apparent there was more than a root attached to it.

"Drop it," Alaric boomed.

Meredith froze as a hawk-like head emerged from the water. The head turned to regard the holder of its tail.

Alaric raced to the water's edge and scooped Meredith off the ground. She released the creature's tail, but it was too late.

"What is it?" Meredith asked.

"I have a theory," I said.

The monster climbed out of the water, revealing the trunk of a lion and the rear of a horse.

"It's a Sak," I said. "A composite of multiple animals."

"Don't forget the lotus tail," Alaric said.

I kept my gaze pinned to the monster. "The fake flower is what reels in its victims."

Meredith closed her eyes and curled against Alaric's chest. "Can we make it go away?"

The creature seemed to realize it was the topic of discussion. Its beak opened and unleashed a horrific sound —high and sharp. If there had been glass nearby, it would have shattered.

The Sak shook off droplets of water and crouched.

Liam rolled up his sleeves. "Looks like our first fight is going to be right here. Sweet."

The prince passed Meredith to me. I would rather be holding my dagger than a child, but there was no time to complain.

The Sak lunged and Alaric rushed to meet it. The vampire grabbed the creature with both arms and squeezed. I'd always known he was strong, but seeing his strength in action was another story.

The Sak thrashed as it tried to escape Alaric's firm embrace. A sharp sound pierced the air again. It seemed like more than a cry of anguish. It seemed like a cry for help. Instinctively I glanced around us. If this guy had friends, we were in trouble.

Alaric hooked an arm around the monster's neck and a loud *crack* followed. The creature slumped to the ground and the prince stepped away.

With a sigh of disappointment, Liam rolled his sleeves back in place. "I guess I'll take the next one."

"We need to go now," I said. "I think that was a summoning cry."

One cue the ground trembled.

Meredith whimpered and clung to my shirt. We should've insisted the children stay behind until the area was clear. The crossing was much too dangerous. Good thing I didn't have kids of my own to protect. I didn't have the instincts needed to be a mother.

"We need to get across the river," Roger said. "Any ideas?"

I glanced skyward. "George, how much weight can you lift?" The dragon would have to take us one at a time, except maybe the children. Still, it shouldn't take very long if we moved quickly.

The pygmy dragon responded by attaching its claws to Liam's shoulders.

"Ouch," the werewolf said. "Time for a manicure, George."

"Wait!" a voice called.

There was a moment of stunned confusion as another figure cut through the shadows.

"I thought you said this was everybody," Liam complained. He shook off George's claws.

The silhouette was female. And familiar.

The tiny hairs on the back of my neck stood at attention. "Meghan?"

"Surprise." She wriggled her fingers.

"What are you doing here?"

"Followed your trail. Wasn't hard. You reek."

Liam sniffed his armpits. "It's the water. I'm having the same issue."

"Who's your friend?" Roger asked.

"She's not my friend. She's here to kill me."

Meghan didn't seem the least bit fazed by my entourage. I couldn't decide whether that made her incredibly brave or incredibly stupid.

"You said you might be able to get me the information I need if I don't kill you," Meghan explained. "So I'm here to not kill you."

Liam pointed behind us. "In case you haven't noticed, we're kind of in the middle of a thing. Can your vendetta wait until after we're done?"

Meghan's gaze drifted past us to the maze in the background. "Are you here to kill monsters?"

"That's the plan," I said.

Her brow creased. "The vampires don't surprise me

since you're clearly in league with them. What's up with the werewolf and the two mini humans?"

"I'm her best friend," Liam said.

"And we're her new friends," Jason added.

Her face registered confusion.

"There are two hundred children descending upon the district within a day or so," I told her. "We're doing what we can to clear the space of monsters so they don't all die. If you want to help, you're welcome to join us. If not, go now before you get yourself killed."

Meghan stood perfectly still as she digested the information. "Are these vampire kids?"

"Humans like us," Meredith said. "And some other kinds, too."

"Orphans," I emphasized.

Meredith slipped around us to stand between our group and Meghan. "Are you a good fighter?"

"I'm pretty good. Ask your friend, Britt. She'll tell you."

Meredith twisted to look at me. "Is she?"

"She held her own," I said.

Meredith turned back to the werewolf. "Okay. You can stay."

Meghan's gaze met mine. "If I help, will you get me the information I want?"

"As long as you agree not to kill me afterward," I said.

The werewolf mulled over the offer.

"Take the deal," Liam urged. "Britt could kill you with her eyes closed if she really wanted to. You're no match for her."

Meghan assessed him. "Is that why you're her friend? Because you're too afraid not to be?"

Liam slung an arm along my shoulders. "I'm her friend

because she saved my life when she didn't even know me, and she makes an excellent bourbon slushie."

Roger looked impressed. "How'd you get your hands on bourbon?"

I peered at Alaric. "I had friends in high places once upon a time."

The ground trembled again beneath our feet.

"It's now or never, Meghan Dunne," I said. "Are you in or out?"

She took a step toward us. "Somebody hand me a weapon."

NINE

One by one George flew us across the river. The pygmy dragon's body sagged by the time Roger's feet touched the ground.

I rubbed his scaled head. "Take a break now. There's more to come." A lot more.

The Lincoln Memorial was the first building within our field of vision. The marble monument seemed mainly intact.

"This is the start of the maze," Roger observed. He pointed to a worn path ahead.

"We could use more light," Jason said. "It seems darker here."

A faint glow grew visible behind the steps of the memorial.

"Are you sure you're not a wizard?" Liam asked the boy. "Maybe a dollop of djinn blood?"

Jason looked mildly alarmed as he shook his head.

The glow increased in size and intensified. By the time it rounded the corner of the monument, it was clear what we were dealing with.

"Flame giant," Roger said, staring at the rising flames that now formed the shape of a giant.

"Oh, wonderful," Liam said. "And here I thought it was just a huge fireball. I feel much better knowing it's a sentient being."

Meghan nudged me. "You're a witch. Can't you conjure a water spell?"

I watched the movements of the fire giant. "Not that kind of witch."

Meghan blew a raspberry. "Looks like you drew the short magic straw."

"Tell me about it," I murmured.

Alaric leaned over and whispered, "Can you manipulate its blood?"

I waved a hand in the direction of the monster. "It's a walking mountain of fire. Where do you think I'll find blood?"

Roger unfastened his cufflinks. "If Alaric and I turn invisible, we can approach from behind while you distract it."

"And do what to it?" I asked. "There's nothing to sink your fangs into."

The flame giant flickered with light and heat as it lumbered toward us.

"I can't blow it up," Liam said with a mixture of surprise and disappointment.

Jason clutched his satchel. "The holy water!"

"I hate to break it to you, but I think you're going to need more water than what's in that vial of yours," Alaric told him.

Ignoring him, Jason opened the satchel and pulled out the antique box. "It might not work on vampires, but that doesn't mean it won't work on flame giants. It's a type of demon." He handed a vial to Roger and one to Alaric. "Sneak attack."

I didn't have any better ideas.

I watched as the two vampires blended with the background.

"Jason, let's go," Liam urged.

The boy remained rooted in place. "Wait. I want to see if my idea works."

I put a hand on the boy's shoulder. "I'll wait with him."

The others started toward the maze.

Jason began to fidget. "The flames aren't getting smaller."

"We can't see what they're doing. Maybe they haven't used the water yet."

The boy's face crumpled as he watched long tendrils smack the ground like fiery whips. "It's attacking them. I have to help. It'll be my fault if they die."

Before I could stop him, he pushed me aside and ran toward the flame giant. My stomach lurched at the sight. That boy was willing to sacrifice himself for the sake of the vampires he wanted to overthrow.

Great gods of old, he deserved to live.

Three flaming whips shot out as Jason approached and left scorch marks on the ground. The boy jumped back, narrowly avoiding injury.

I sprinted toward him.

"Get back. There's nothing you can do." I shoved my way in front of him.

The boy must've tripped because he yanked the back of my vest hard. I fell backward. My funny bone hit the ground, sending a shooting pain along my arm.

Although the flame giant had no eyes, I could tell the precise moment it zeroed in on me.

"Jason, go!"

A tendril lashed out and smacked my leg. The patch of material sizzled and disintegrated.

I didn't care if my whole leg burned, as long as the boy was safe.

As another tendril sailed toward me, I rolled to the side and jumped to my feet. Jason was still there, paralyzed by fear. "Come on, Jason. Let's help the others."

He didn't need to be told twice. We turned and ran together. I wanted to put as much distance between us and the giant as possible. Its slow speed might be our saving grace.

We arrived at a rectangular body of water. It was covered in dark green film. From here we could still see the glow of flames.

"The giant is shrinking," Meredith declared.

She was right. It was.

Jason pumped a fist in the air.

I continued to watch from a safe distance for any sign of Alaric and Roger. Finally their silhouettes appeared against the background of a dying star. A black hole formed in the flame giant's middle and spread until the figure merged with the night.

"Well done, you two," Liam said. "Shiny gold star to both of you." He paused. "Too soon?"

"We could use more light," Jason said.

Liam clamped a hand over the boy's mouth.

Roger returned the two vials to Jason. "I don't know what was in there, but it was potent."

"Maybe you were wrong," I said to Alaric. "Maybe the water could kill vampires."

"Then the two of us would be dead already," he replied.

"Operation Monster Maze, phase two," Jason said. He pivoted toward the entrance to the maze.

"Somebody's feeling confident," Alaric murmured.

As long as his confidence didn't get him killed, I was all for it.

"On your left," Liam yelled.

I heard the vicious snarl before the creature came into view. A hulking figure on two legs covered in coarse brown hair. Two horns protruded from its enormous head.

A minotaur.

I'd crossed paths with one before, in the Pocono Mountains before my servitude. Minotaurs were dangerous because of their strength, so I'd wisely hidden behind a boulder until it passed. There were no boulders here. Nowhere to hide seven trespassers. The city had been largely demolished by Mother Nature and monsters, which was one reason The White House stood out like a beacon in the night. It was one of the few buildings here from pre-Eternal Night still standing and reasonably intact.

Alaric launched himself at the creature. As the vampire wrestled the beast to the ground, I caught a glimpse of movement directly north of us. At least I thought so. The shadows were still now.

While I was distracted by movement, Meghan had shifted and joined Alaric in the fight. Her jaws snapped around the minotaur's leg and the beast moaned as blood seeped from the wound.

"Do you guys need me?" Liam called, giving his bag a shake. "I have explosives."

I urged the children to stay behind me. The air grew quiet as the minotaur drew its last breath. Just as Alaric returned to his feet, I heard the eerie sound of hooves hitting the pavement.

It wasn't over yet.

The next minotaur followed on the heels of the first, this one running toward us on all fours. Its nostrils blew steam. We may as well have been waving a red flag.

Still in wolf form, Meghan intercepted the monster. Her powerful jaws clamped down on the creature's shoulder. Alaric seized the opportunity to wrap his arms around the beast's neck and twist.

Roger raised a finger. "Are you sure you don't need any help?"

Alaric wiped blood from his shirt. "We're good."

The vampire was in his element. I was so accustomed to seeing him with a drink in his hand and a woman on his arm —this new Alaric was wholly unexpected.

It seemed I didn't know the royal vampire as well I believed.

Meredith's scream alerted us to new danger. I spun around to see a third minotaur gunning for us. I pushed the children aside. I wasn't strong enough to overpower a minotaur, but I'd amassed a number of survival skills in my youth.

"Stop the blood flow!" Roger shouted.

I didn't have time to form a connection and Alaric still had my gun. I withdrew my daggers and stood my ground. As the creature reared up on hind legs, I jumped, sticking both blades in the chest and slicing straight down to its testicles. As my boots landed on the ground, guts spilled forth like angry worms. The monster fell forward and I heard the crunch of bones as it hit the earth.

"They just keep coming," Roger said. "How many do you think there are?"

My gaze swept the murky landscape and a piece of the

monster puzzle clicked into place. "They're coming from the same direction."

"No, they're not." Roger formed a V with his arms. "The minotaurs came from two different directions."

"Yes, but I spotted the second minotaur there before it attacked us from this side." I pointed north. "I think the monsters are starting at the same spot."

Roger seemed to ponder my idea. "Their own entrance to the maze."

Alaric squinted into the gloaming. "What's that large building up ahead?"

"I don't know what it is now, but it used to be The White House," Roger said.

"Where the human leader of the United Territories lived?" Meredith asked.

"The United States of America," I corrected her. "I think that's where we want to go."

Meghan snorted. "Why would we want to go where there's a concentration of monsters?"

Liam patted his bag. "I can think of one reason."

"I think someone is sending them through the maze from there," I said.

"How could someone control all these monsters?" Meghan asked, unconvinced.

I looked at her. "Think about it. Why haven't the monsters spread from the Wasteland? There's no ward locking them in. They can cross the river. There's no reason for them not to stray from the district, yet they don't leave. Something or someone must be keeping them here."

"The monsters are someone's security system," Roger said.

"Kill the puppeteer, stop the puppets," Alaric murmured.

I nodded.

"Who would be powerful enough to control all these monsters?" the prince asked.

"Only one way to find out." I chose the path to the left but stopped when I realized the children were following. I swiveled to face them. "You need to stay here. It's too dangerous." I looked up at the pygmy dragon. "You, too, George."

Meghan drew the children closer to her. "I'll stay with them."

Roger glanced from The White House to us. "I'll stay, too."

"I'm coming," Liam said. "Somebody better need me soon. I postponed a hot date for this rendezvous."

I raised an eyebrow. "A date?"

"Remember that guy Kenny I met at work?"

"Oh, wow. I thought he wasn't interested."

"I thought so, too." The werewolf shrugged. "Apparently I'm terrible at reading signals."

Alaric withdrew the Monster Masher from the back of his pants and gave it to Roger. "In case you need protection while you're waiting."

I linked arms with Liam. "We're off to see The Wizard," I sang.

Alaric observed the path of the maze. "Follow the Yellow Brick Road?"

"Let's hope if we see a lion, it's cowardly," Liam remarked.

"Are you sure you're up for this?" I asked my friend. "You can stay with the others."

Liam scoffed. "In the kiddie section? I don't think so."

Roger waved. "Have fun storming the castle."

"Wrong movie, but good effort," I called.

The White House wasn't as intact as it appeared from a distance. One side of the building had crumbled and the roof had partially collapsed. Remnants of a fence were visible along the left perimeter.

"What's the plan?" Liam asked.

I spared him a glance. "What makes you think there's a plan?"

"We're marching into the heart of enemy territory. You wouldn't do that without a plan, would you?" He observed me for a moment. "You absolutely would. Shit. I'm an idiot."

"Not too late to turn back," Alaric advised.

Liam puffed out his chest. "I'm good. I may look like an engineer on the outside, but inside..." He scratched the back of his head. "Inside I'm an engineer, too."

Alaric clapped him on the back. "Good. We can use skills like yours."

Hope shone in the werewolf's eyes. "Really?"

"No. I just wanted to make you feel better. Did it work?"

Liam's expression crumpled and I stifled a laugh.

The werewolf shifted his focus to the dilapidated building. "What kind of creature do you think is powerful enough to control all these other monsters?"

"My money's on a vampire," Alaric said.

I grunted. "Naturally."

"What? There are legends about ancient vampires that still walk among us."

"With a cane, maybe."

"What kind of vampire would want to rule the Wasteland?" Liam asked.

"One incapable of ruling a House," Alaric replied.

I wasn't convinced. Vampires ruled the world, but this

area...The Wasteland was like another planet. Vampires could be in charge of any territory they wanted. I agreed with Liam—the district seemed like an odd choice.

The interior of the White House was less gloomy than the exterior. There were too many rooms to count.

"Where do we start?" Alaric asked. "This place isn't exactly prepped to receive visitors."

I was beginning to think our theory was wrong.

"There's a bunker," Liam offered. "Maybe we should check there."

I looked at him askance. "What's a bunker?"

"Humans used them as underground hideaways for protection during a dangerous event."

Alaric wore a wry smile. "Like ten supervolcanoes erupting at the same time?"

"Something like that. Before the Great Eruption, The White House allegedly built a huge bunker to accommodate the president and their staff in case of a nuclear war."

"A bunker in a government hub would have weapons and controls," Alaric said.

I found it hard to believe anybody would choose to live underground. It was a foreign concept in a world where you put your life at risk every time you ventured below ground. Even riding the subway was fraught with danger. It didn't stop everyone from doing it, but a high percentage of the population wouldn't dream of setting foot down there. I knew other places that were worse than New York. From what I'd been told, Britannia City had a sprawling underground system that was swarming with monsters and criminals. No thanks.

"Find the bunker, find the puppet master," Liam said.

I didn't love the idea of searching a bunker. What if the

puppet master shut us inside? We'd be lost forever and no one would know what happened to us.

Then I thought of the horde of children marching to the Wasteland and I knew I had to take the chance.

"Any idea where the entrance to this bunker might be?" Alaric asked.

"I have an idea."

Leave it to the engineer. We let Liam take the lead. He guided us to the eastern wing of the building. We walked in and out of several rooms with Liam sniffing the air until he found the one he wanted. We entered through a nondescript door and down a flight of stairs where we were met by a set of steel doors.

Alaric nudged the large door open. "I guess we're going in. Liam, go back upstairs and wait for us."

"Wait, what? I don't even get to see it?" Liam's voice cracked slightly as it tended to do when he got worked up over an issue. The issue didn't have to be important. I once heard his voice crack because he failed to get the last banana in the fruit bowl.

"We need someone to wait in case someone tries to come down. We don't know how many adversaries we'll face here," I explained.

Liam seemed to accept the decision. "Fine, but I'm preparing for battle." He dropped his backpack to the floor and unzipped it.

Alaric put a finger to his lips and we ventured through the doors, entering a subterranean hall. The tile on the floor was old and broken. Rotting pipes hung from the ceiling. Then we arrived at an anteroom and everything changed.

The bunker was not what I pictured. Underground in New York City was dirtier and darker than aboveground. Nobody wanted to spend time below ground unless absolutely necessary. Not the case here. It looked like someone had taken all the best pieces from the main floor and moved them down here to create their own underground paradise. The furniture and artwork were well-preserved and there were offshoots to other rooms.

"This bunker is massive," Alaric whispered.

"I think it spans the length and width of the building." It seemed to encompass the entire footprint of the former White House. Whether it had always been that way was unclear.

"We stay together," Alaric insisted. "This place is just as much of a maze as outside."

He was right. If we lost each other down here…It was best not to think about the possibility.

Alaric pointed to the larger corridor to the left. "Let's start this way."

We quickly discovered 'this way' was a containment center. Each individual cell held a monster. Some were empty. They likely belonged to the creatures we encountered outside. The doors opened at the back of the cells, which meant there was an underground tunnel that led to the outdoors so the monsters didn't come through the bunker or the building. Made sense.

I walked past each cell, casting a wary eye on every monster along the way. More minotaurs. A serpent the size of a horse with a spiked tail. I halted in front of a cell with what appeared to be a young woman. She sat in the corner with her arms wrapped around her shins and her knees tucked up to her chest. Her forehead was pressed to her knees so she didn't notice me.

I motioned to Alaric. "What do you think? Siren?"

The vampire examined the woman behind the glass.

"Hard to tell. I can't smell through whatever this material is."

The young woman must've sensed our presence because she lifted her face. Her eyes were red from crying. When she spotted us, she quickly wiped away her tears. If she was a monster, she was the saddest, most self-aware monster I'd ever seen.

I offered a friendly wave and Alaric gently smacked my arm.

"Why did you wave?"

I looked at him askance. "What? I don't want to frighten her."

"She's the one in the containment cell. Maybe we're the ones who should be frightened."

I beckoned her forward. She pointed to herself with an expression of surprise.

"Yes, you," Alaric said, sounding slightly mystified. "Who else?"

The young woman crawled across the floor of the cell and kneeled in front of us. I couldn't tell if she was injured or had been contained so long that her leg muscles had atrophied. Her brown hair was loose and a little mussed, but relatively shiny and clean. She wore a long-sleeved red shirt and black pants, neither of which were stained or ripped. Her feet were bare. I was starting to wonder if she was a recent captive.

Her mouth moved, but the sound didn't reach us. I wasn't surprised the cells were soundproof. If she'd been a siren, she could've persuaded someone to free her long before now.

She seemed to realize we couldn't hear her because she pointed to our right. She jabbed her finger repeatedly and her brown eyes radiated desperation.

"I think she's trying to tell us where the controls are," I said.

"Even if we find them, how will we know which button is for her cell? I don't see any way to identify them."

"One step at a time."

I held up a finger to the young woman to let her know we'd be back in a minute. My gut told me she was human. Didn't mean she wasn't a monster, of course—I'd met my share of them in human form—but it seemed more likely that she'd been captured by a madman.

We crept forward, even managing to ignore the monster self-flagellating with his tongue.

"I'm equal parts disgusted and jealous," Alaric whispered as we continued onward.

Finally Monster Hall emptied us into another room shaped like a hexagon. Dozens of screens covered one wall. Upon closer inspection, I realized they were feeds from security cameras set up around the district. I spotted Roger in the corner of one of the screens. Another camera showed the rectangular pond we passed on the way here.

"Do you see any controls for the cells?" I asked, tearing my attention away from the screen.

"Not yet." Alaric was also stuck on the security footage. There seemed to be a camera at every entry point to the Wasteland. The only chance of a successful sneak attack would be knowing when the control center was unmanned, like right now.

A round marble table took pride of place in the heart of the hexagon. On top of the table was a scrying glass. It was larger than any I'd seen before—bigger than a dragon's egg and probably ten times as heavy. As I approached the table, I noticed swirls of different colors moving across the globe.

"I think we've found the control panel," I said.

Alaric moved closer to examine the orb. "That thing? I thought it was for show."

"No, it's fully functional." I sensed the magic contained within it.

He leaned over the table. "How do you use it?"

"I'm not sure we can." Worth a try, though. I placed both hands on the scrying glass and said, "Show me the young woman in the cell."

I watched as the swirls merged and then pulled apart to reveal the brunette in the cell. She was exactly where we'd left her.

I kept my hands on the orb and felt the glass grow warm against my skin. "Release the young woman in the cell."

The sound of clapping startled me and I jerked my hands to my sides.

"Well done, witch."

I pivoted to see a white-bearded man in a red tracksuit. His long white hair was secured in a ponytail down his back.

"Santa called. He wants his look back."

The man laughed and his eyes crinkled at the corners. Great gods, he was even jolly. He wasn't overweight though. The Eternal Night took care of the obesity problem that had plagued humankind before the Great Eruption.

I now held a dagger ready in each hand. If nothing else it would make my opponent think weapons were my best option. "What's your name?"

Santa turned to me, still wearing a slightly amused and condescending expression. It made me want to hurl both daggers at his face. "You'll never believe me."

"Kris Kringle?" I guessed.

"Santana."

"Huh."

"What's with the monster maze?" Alaric demanded. "Is this where you control them?"

He beamed with pride. "Amazing place, isn't it? I've spent years perfecting it."

"For what purpose?" I asked.

"To keep everyone out, of course. Become the ruler of my own kingdom." He looked at Alaric. "You don't mind, do you? You have so much land. You can't possibly miss this little slice of heaven."

"How do you know who I am?" Alaric asked.

"Think of me as the Wizard of Oz."

"The Wizard of Oz was a phony who didn't know anything," I pointed out.

Santana scratched his beard. "Right. Not a good analogy. How about Sauron? He had the all-seeing eye, didn't he?"

Alaric flicked the scrying glass. "Are you a seer?"

"A wizard. My spells include one of foresight."

"You use magic to see the future?" I pressed.

"Among other things." The wizard offered Alaric an apologetic smile. "I realize I'm admitting to a capital offense. Please be merciful."

There was a mocking quality in his tone. Alaric must've sensed it, too, because his jaw tightened and his hands balled into fists.

Santana walked to the other side of the table and placed a protective hand on the glass. "I've seen so much in this globe. You have no idea."

"Like what?" I prompted.

A sly smile emerged. "Like you and your friends fighting my pets, among other things. It's been ages since I've enjoyed that much entertainment. I might invite more visitors now that I know how fun it can be."

"Is that what happened to your pretty friend in the cell?" I asked. "She wandered too close to your maze so you decided to invite her to join you permanently?"

"Twila is my assistant. She's currently serving out a punishment for insubordination. I'll let her go in..." He consulted an imaginary watch. "Two more days."

I had a feeling Twila would rather drown herself in the Potomac than stay another day as Santana's assistant.

With preternatural speed, Alaric grabbed the scrying glass from the table and held it aloft, ready to smash it to bits.

Santana threw up his hands. "Wait, you don't want to do that."

"Give me one good reason," Alaric said.

"For starters, its destruction will result in the release of all the monsters from their cells. I don't think you want to do that when your friends are so vulnerable." He motioned to the screens, which currently showed Roger engaged in conversation with the children. Meghan stared past them, keeping careful watch. George hovered above them all, looking irritated to be left behind.

"Okay, that's a pretty good reason," Alaric mumbled. He lowered the glass but continued to hold it.

"Then we'll just take it with us so you can't use it anymore," I suggested.

Santana's laughter was condescending. "That won't do either, I'm afraid. Why don't we make a deal? You put back the globe and I'll tell you the secrets it's already revealed to me."

"What kind of secrets?" I asked.

The wizard wiggled his fingers. "The scrying glass first."

"No dice." Alaric held the globe against his chest.

"I know why you're here and where you're headed," Santana said.

Alaric eyed him with suspicion. "Do you know why?

"Your father has been murdered and your mother hired this one to escort you safely home." The wizard turned to me. "Marvelous job so far, by the way, although this little detour was a grave miscalculation on your part."

I didn't disagree.

Alaric seemed more alarmed than impressed. "How do you know about my father? Who are you working with—House Nilsson?"

The wizard made a dismissive sound. "As if I would align myself with vampires of any House. Do you think someone like me who's managed to survive unimpeded for so long would stoop to licking the boots of depraved monsters?"

Alaric's eyes blazed with indignant fury. He wanted to smash the globe just to spite the wizard, I could feel it.

"Alaric, why don't you put down the globe?" I suggested. The last thing we needed was a Wasteland full of uncontrollable monsters. We'd make a bad situation even worse.

I tried to steer the conversation away from vampire insults. "Must've been rough to watch your pets die. Maybe you should stop this whole dog-and-pony show to avoid more casualties."

"I'd say it will be rougher for you to watch each other die." He thrust a hand toward Alaric, cupping his fingers. The vampire froze against his will and Santana took the scrying glass from his rigid hands.

Not. Good.

Most wizards and witches excelled in one specific type of magic—elementals mastered water, for example, while others specialized in fire. Some were telekinetic or adept at mind control. Santana seemed to excel in spells, which was more dangerous because a skilled magic user could create a spell to accomplish just about anything. I had no desire to find out exactly how skilled Santana was.

The wizard flicked his wrist and Alaric went sailing across the room against his will. The prince slammed into the wall and slumped to the floor.

I focused on the wizard and tried to forge a connection with his blood. Similar to what happened with Vincent, something was blocking my access.

Santana clucked his tongue. "Not so fast, witch. I'm afraid your access has been denied."

He opened his palm in my direction. Before his spell reached me, I pricked my finger and watched drops of my blood hit the floor in front of me, effectively blocking his spell.

The wizard scowled. "You waste your time here when there are greater games afoot."

"We're saving hundreds of innocent lives," I shot back. "I don't consider that a waste of time."

"The lives of human children aren't worth the spit shine on my shoes. The Fallen can only be replaced by a species strong enough to survive."

There was a definite whiff of 'a species like ours' packed into his statement.

I spread my arms wide. "Then I guess we've reached an impasse because I'm not leaving until I know the kids can live here safely."

"There's no such thing as safely. Not for them. Not for us." The wizard's gaze slid to my left. "And certainly not for him."

I spared a glance over my shoulder to see Alaric staggering back to his feet.

"That spell should've held you longer," the wizard said. "No matter. Where one man sees failure, I see opportunity."

"Maybe you're not as powerful as you think," Alaric said in a voice that would've given me nightmares if I hadn't known him.

"I guess we'll see about that when you meet my prototype. I've been training him for combat in the war to come."

I frowned. "The war against House August?"

"The war against *all* Houses." Santana seemed almost giddy at the prospect.

"We're more interested in the war that's imminent," I said.

"I'm afraid there isn't much you can do to stop it. Ironic that House Nilsson isn't to blame. Two great Houses will tear each other to pieces for nothing."

"Not for nothing," Alaric snarled. "For the murder of my father."

Santana leveled a look at the vampire. "Except House Nilsson had nothing to do with the assassination of King Maxwell."

My head started to spin. "If not them, then who?"

Smiling faintly, the wizard placed the orb on the table. "Let's all welcome Frank to the party."

A door slid open on the floor to reveal a secret chamber beneath us. A figure rose from the bowels of the bunker. He had a body like a tree trunk and was so tall that the top of his head skimmed the ceiling. Three eyes—one in the middle and two on either temple, presumably for advanced peripheral vision. He sported six limbs, each extension ending with a weapon designed to kill a vampire. They were the same on both sides—a hatchet, a stake, and a longsword.

Santana pivoted to face the prince. "Why don't the two of you get acquainted, then you can tell me again how I'm not as powerful as I think?"

The creature moved to stand between us, effectively blocking my path to Alaric. With nothing but solid wall behind him and a multi-limbed, armed monster in front of him, the prince was trapped.

Santana motioned to the exit. "You're free to leave, witch. I'd like to give you a chance to reconsider where your loyalties lie. We could use someone with your skills in the days ahead."

I watched Alaric take his first swing at the monster. The creature didn't flinch.

My heart pounded.

The vampire turned invisible, but one of the creature's arms lashed out and the stake made contact, ending the vampire's invisibility. He was hunched over, trying to stop the blood from gushing from his side.

If Alaric died, House August would surely fall. I'd live to see another day and I'd gain my freedom even without the queen's permission.

Still, I couldn't let him die. Whether he cared for me or not didn't matter. Yes, he was a smug and arrogant bastard and had treated me like I was a number with genitals, but I wasn't Santana and I certainly wasn't one of the monsters in the maze.

"Last chance, witch," Santana said. He had the scrying glass tucked under his arm and was preparing to vacate the hexagon.

I had a feeling there was a set of airtight doors that would close behind him, leaving us to our fates.

I made a show of turning toward the monster.

"Very well then," the wizard said.

I tried to forge a connection with Frank's blood, although it wouldn't be easy. The wizard had used a mix of creatures' blood, which seemed to confuse my magic. I was having trouble latching on.

Alaric remained upright, but his face was damp with sweat and there were patches of blood on the floor.

I made another attempt to connect. Tendrils of magic slid over and through the blood, identifying its cells and platelets. I detected the blood of a dragon, as well as an ogre, a wizard, and a human. I suspected the wizard blood was his own.

"I won't let you hurt anyone else," a shrill voice yelled.

I twisted to see Twila rush forward and hurl herself at the wizard. Although I lost the connection to Frank, I took advantage of the distraction and grabbed the scrying glass from the wizard's grasp. It was as heavy as it looked and I nearly dropped it. Santana shoved the girl to the floor and raised a hand to me. Instinctively I held the glass in front of me to block the magic. Santana's spell ricocheted off the orb and shot back at him. The wizard's body sparked and his red suit began to smoke. Whatever he'd tried to do to me, it wasn't gentle.

His body seized and his eyes rolled back in his head. He tried to grab the edge of the table, but his hand slipped and he fell backward.

Twila stared in horror.

"There's a guy named Liam upstairs," I told her. "Get him."

She turned and ran. It helped that she was accustomed to taking orders.

I swiveled back to the monster that currently had Alaric

pinned to the wall with two swords stuck through the fabric of his shirt. The creature drew back the arm with a hatchet, ready to wield the fatal blow.

I concentrated on the blood I'd already identified. There was no time for gentle maneuvering. I had to act.

My magic seeped into the creature's blood and I yanked as hard as I could. His arm stopped mid-motion, leaving the hatchet a hair's breadth from Alaric's neck.

I'd been planning to slow the monster's blood to put him to sleep, but instead I seemed to be...controlling him. I kept my grip on the blood and *pulled*.

The extended arms pulled back, releasing their hold on the vampire. He dropped to the floor, clutching his side.

I watched in amazement as I forced the monster to abandon his prey. Frank lumbered to the side of the hexagon. I held on to his blood, unwilling to release him yet. My breathing was ragged from exertion. I'd never controlled my target before—had never tried—let alone a target with multiple bloodlines. The implications were more than I could handle.

I was a greater threat than even *I* realized.

Liam appeared in the entryway alongside Twila. "Is it time to blow things up?"

"Set up, then we need to help Alaric. He's hurt."

While Liam put his incendiary devices to good use, I maintained my focus on Frank, pumping his blood and urging him toward the secret chamber. It required more energy and magic than what I was used to expending. Only when the door was sealed above his head did I dare withdraw my magic. I sucked in a deep breath and spun toward the werewolf.

"What in the hell was that thing?" Liam asked.

"Later."

I hurried to Alaric. Liam and I each hooked an arm underneath the vampire's shoulders and dragged him all the way out of the bunker.

"Twila, we need to go," I called over my shoulder to the assistant. She lingered at the base of the steps, as though uncertain what to do next. She hugged the scrying glass to her chest.

"If you stay, you die," Liam said. "Nothing in this bunker will make it out alive."

Looking up at us, Twila swallowed hard. "Promise?"

# TEN

The explosives detonated.

The sound was deafening but even worse was the blast itself. It propelled us forward to the front lawn of The White House along with debris, and I lost sight of my companions in the haze of smoke.

I crawled on my hands and knees through the wreckage screaming Alaric's name. I found him behind a pile of metal and wood. He was bruised and bloody but alive.

His gaze snagged mine. "You saved me," he murmured.

"That's my job, remember?" I pointed to myself. "Knight in shiny leather armor."

"You could've left me to die. It would've solved all your problems in one fell swoop."

I shrugged. "Change of heart."

His fingers skimmed my jawline. "No. I don't think there's been a change at all."

"There you are!" Liam burst through the debris like a minotaur in a china shop with Twila right behind him. "And here I thought I might find two corpses."

Alaric struggled to his feet. "Feeling disappointed?"

"Not at all. I'm thrilled to not have to find my way back through the maze alone. I left a trail of breadcrumbs, but I'm pretty sure the birds ate it."

"Birds?" Alaric queried.

My stomach gurgled. "Wait. You had bread?"

Liam offered a sheepish grin. "It was my emergency stash. I'm more of a protein guy than a carbs guy, but bread was preferable to starvation." He pointed to Alaric's bloody shirt. "That's quite a gash you've got there."

Alaric pressed his hands to his wound.

"We need to get you to a healer," I said.

He shook his head. "It's already healing. I can feel it."

The prince was fine. Totally and completely fine. The realization was exhilarating.

"Thank you," Twila said. "I know you weren't here to save me, but..." She ducked her head. "I thought no one would ever come."

I couldn't imagine the horrors she'd endured.

"So are we done here?" Liam asked, injecting a hopeful note into his voice. "Can we go home?"

"Done here, yes," I said. "Going home is a different story."

The werewolf gripped the ends of his hair and groaned. "I was afraid you were going to say that. What's the plan now?"

"We learned something about the king's death," I said and proceeded to explain what the wizard had revealed.

Liam's eyes grew wider with each new statement. "A battle between two vampire Houses? That's not how I want to die." He shot a glance at Alaric. "No offense, Your Highness."

"It isn't how I want to die either," Alaric said.

"Let's get back to the others and figure out next steps," I

said. We'd regroup and, if necessary, go our separate ways. I didn't expect Liam and Meghan to follow us. This wasn't their fight. Technically it wasn't mine either, except that I'd pledged to return the prince safely to New York. If that meant helping him stop a war, then so be it.

As we made our way back through the maze, my brain was in overdrive. I was confused by my newfound ability. I'd killed targets. I'd rendered them unconscious. But I'd never controlled their actions. I'd never thought to try. And to be able to control Frank's multiple bloodlines at once suggested that I could control multiple targets simultaneously.

We arrived at the rectangular pond near the Lincoln Memorial where our party awaited us. Meredith and Jason broke into matching smiles at the sight of us. I felt conflicted about leaving the children on their own in the Wasteland. On the one hand, they'd traveled hundreds of miles without adult supervision. On the other hand, they were planning to settle here. They'd need infrastructure, supplies—all sorts of things they didn't currently have and wouldn't have the means to acquire.

Roger's eyebrows crept up to his hairline. "Your Highness, you look...tired."

Meghan snorted. "More like skewered."

I decided to give a voice to my thoughts. "I'm worried about leaving these kids so soon. There might be a few stray monsters lurking."

Twila shifted the scrying glass to rest on a hip. "I was a teacher before Santana tricked me into coming here. I could stay and help."

Roger seemed to notice her for the first time. "Who are you?"

"Twila. Executive Assistant to a Madman."

Roger nodded vaguely. "I sort of get that vibe."

"Once we return to the compound, I'll send help," Alaric offered.

I shot him a quizzical look. "You'd do that? Why?"

"Because they're children." His lips melted into a smile. "Damn tough ones at that. They deserve a chance to build their own world."

"The district is in House August territory and the children have expressed their desire to overthrow vampire rule. If you look the other way, it'll be viewed as a weakness," I said.

"My father's death is a bigger weakness." He touched my arm and every cell in my body reacted. "We have other battles to fight right now, Britt."

We certainly did.

"What if I stayed, too?" Liam asked.

I looked at him. "What about New York?"

"In New York I'm..." He scratched the back of his head as he cast an awkward glance at the prince. "I'm a wolf that submits. For once I'd like to know what it feels like to be in charge of a pack." He shrugged. "Even if it's a pack of pint-sized humans."

I understood.

Liam looked at the prince. "I work on behalf of House August. The one who can offer me dispensation to head this special task force is right here."

Alaric didn't hesitate. "An engineer will be useful to them."

The werewolf grinned from ear to ear. "I've always wanted to be Peter Pan to the Lost Boys. This will be our Neverland."

"Just make sure the waters are clear of crocs." Neverland might have a crocodile with a ticking clock, but in this world, it would be a three-headed crocodile the size of a city block and no early warning system.

I felt better leaving Liam in charge. Despite his fascination with explosives, he was a solid guy to have around and I knew he'd do his best to look after the children.

Roger cast a speculative glance across the darkened district. "How would you feel about me staying, too?"

Alaric balked. "Here? What about Palm Beach? I need someone there."

"They need me here more." Roger waved a hand at the Wasteland. "You know I'm very organized. I can help rebuild this place from the ground up. I promise to head back to Palm Beach as soon as things settle here."

"There are a lot of kids," I said.

Alaric clapped his friend on the shoulder. "I appreciate the gesture, but I need you in the Southern Territories. I'm afraid that's an order."

Meghan shifted on the balls of her feet. "I might hang around and help out, at least for a few days. It's not like I have anywhere I need to be until…" She fixed me with a meaningful look.

Now that her thirst for revenge had been quenched, Meghan needed a new focus. Maybe the children would provide one.

Not wanting to be left out of the conversation, George flapped his wings.

"Not to worry," I said. "No one's asking you to stay. If you want to stick with us, you can."

The pygmy dragon flew a couple loops to express his delight.

"Keep in touch, B," Liam urged. "I want to know you're safe and sound."

I patted the phone in my pocket. "Emergency use only."

Meredith threw her arms around my waist and squeezed. "Thank you. Thank you. Thank you."

I held her, feeling slightly uncomfortable. It wasn't often I had a child's arms around me. Or ever.

"Best of luck, Jason," Alaric said, pumping the boy's hand. "I know we're leaving the Wasteland in good hands."

Alaric and I separated from the group and returned to the minivan.

"I can't believe it's exactly where I left it," he said. "I thought for sure it would be stolen for scraps."

I slid behind the wheel and Alaric settled beside me. George sprawled across the backseat.

Alaric leaned his head against the seat and grinned. "Just like old times."

"Not quite." I debated whether to reveal my newly discovered ability.

No. I couldn't risk it. What if they used it as an excuse not to grant my freedom? I had to keep it to myself.

We made it as far as Baltimore without incident.

"Two hundred miles to go," Alaric commented. "Should we stop here to rest and then push to reach home tomorrow?"

My bottom was still sore from my bike ride, not that I'd admit it to Alaric. "Sounds like a plan."

"I'll send a message to my mother."

"What will it say? A crazy wizard told us House Nilsson is innocent. Please don't attack them or the world will end. XOXO, Prince Alaric."

"Don't be ridiculous," he said. "I wouldn't sign a note to my mother from Prince Alaric. Just Alaric. Or maybe Your Loving Son."

I rolled my eyes. "She won't believe you, not without proof."

"I know, but I'd still rather try and do something until I can speak to her in person. If she attacks House Nilsson, North America will descend into chaos."

"It's a risk to you, Alaric. What if someone intercepts the message to her and figures out where you are?"

"We're not staying in one spot. We're forging ahead, remember?"

I yawned. "Trust me. I remember. Two hours of sleep for you and then two hours for me. Then we'll carry on."

He frowned. "It isn't enough. We'll end up pushing ourselves too hard and collapse by the time we reach the city limits."

"And then we rest."

His face darkened. "No. Then we fight."

At Baltimore's inner harbor, we stopped in front of a sculpture dedicated to the Great Eruption. Ten metal rings were linked together but set at varying heights. The base was a block of concrete painted brown and green.

Alaric shook his head. "I'll never understand modern art."

"How can you not see it?" I pointed to the first ring. "La Garita Caldera." That one spanned Colorado, Utah, and Nevada. "Second ring represents Lake Toba in North Sumatra. Third ring is Cerro Guacha, the Miocene caldera in southwestern Bolivia."

Alaric chuckled. "You're making this up."

I glared at him. "Of course not. Don't they teach you royal vampires anything aside from how to look good holding a goblet of blood?"

He smirked. "You think I look good holding a goblet of blood?"

"You're missing the point." I continued identifying the rings. "Fourth ring is Yellowstone Caldera in Wyoming.

Fifth ring is Lake Taupo on what was once the North Island of New Zealand. Sixth ring is Cerro Galán in Argentina. Seventh is Island Park Caldera that crosses the borders of Idaho and Wyoming. The eighth ring is Vilama, the Miocene caldera in Bolivia and Argentina. The ninth ring is La Pacana, the Miocene age caldera in Chile."

"And the tenth ring is Pastos Grandes in Bolivia," Alaric finished. "See, I do know something."

These ten rings represented death and destruction. An unprecedented global catastrophe that was neither foreseen nor preventable. The cloud of ash from the eruption expanded to coat the earth's atmosphere, wreaking havoc. The world struggled in the face of such drastic changes. The vampires climbed to the top of the food chain. They commandeered witches and wizards to create a magical infrastructure that kept plants alive and prevented mass extinction. They weren't being altruistic, of course. They needed humans alive to serve as their primary food source, which meant keeping the population fed and giving them a will to live. According to the vampires I knew, human blood tasted better when then there was no coercion or distress, so they lulled them into a false sense of security and won their cooperation.

The rings were a beautiful monument in honor of a dark and depressing time. I was glad I wasn't alive at the start. My own upbringing had been difficult enough. I wasn't sure I had the stones for anything worse.

We left the harbor and found an abandoned building on the outskirts of the city. A motel was too risky. The closer we got to New York, the more likely the prince would be recognized.

"Now's a good time to find food," I told George. "Meet us back here in two hours."

The pygmy dragon flew off.

"I don't mind taking first watch," Alaric said. "You must've used more energy back there taking on the wizard and the freak."

"No, I'll do it. You sleep." I didn't want to let on that I needed to rest more than usual. It would raise too many questions.

When he decided to use my lap as a pillow, I didn't object. It was kind of sweet. I resisted the desire to run my fingers through his hair. I still remembered the way it felt against my skin. Smooth and soft like silk. I cleared my throat and adjusted my position without disturbing him. Even though we were in the middle of an abandoned building in a foreign city, I felt comfortable seated here with Alaric's head resting on me. Natural.

*Get it together, Britt.* I wasn't here on a romantic getaway. I was here to protect the prince's life.

After his time was up, we swapped places.

"Feel free to put your face in my lap," he said with a devilish grin.

"Your shoulder will do."

He chuckled as I reconfigured my body to rest against his. I'd end up with a kink in my neck but better than behaving in a way I'd soon regret.

My bizarre dream involved minotaurs bowling with scrying glasses. I awoke to Alaric jostling me and I thought my time was up.

"We've got company," he whispered when he saw my eyes open.

I bolted upright. "Where?"

He pointed to the partial wall across the room.

"Species?"

"They scented us, so I'm going with wolf."

A white wolf proved him right, leaping over the partial wall. Our new friend was followed by a second wolf with a shaggy brown coat. More wolves spilled into the space from every direction.

"This must be their turf," I said.

I held up my hands and rose to my feet. "We're just passing through. We didn't realize this place was yours."

A dozen wolves fanned around us now, baring their teeth and snarling.

"We're not looking for a fight," I insisted. "We only stopped to rest."

A man climbed over the partial wall and entered the building. His shaggy brown hair matched the coat of the second wolf and I had no doubt they were related.

"We're happy to help you rest, Your Highness." He gazed at the vampire with a predatory intensity. "Permanently."

"You know who I am?" the prince asked.

"Why do you think we're here?" He extended a hand to me. "Consider yourself liberated, witch."

My stomach tightened. What was happening? "Who are you?"

"I'm Emil. My pack and I are part of the resistance."

Alaric laughed. "Ah, another resistance group. How many are we up to now—five hundred and three?"

Emil growled. "We're here to overthrow vampires, starting with you, Your Highness."

Alaric's nostrils flared. "I don't think so."

Emil's amber eyes fixed on me. "Let's go, princess. We don't have all day."

My gaze flicked from the werewolf to Alaric. Once again, the universe was presenting me with an opportunity to leave. A path to freedom.

And once again, I found myself declining to trade Alaric's life for it.

I locked eyes with Emil and forced my way into his bloodstream. My magic nestled in his veins allowing me to slow the flow of his blood.

The werewolf shifted uncomfortably. "What are you doing?"

"Taking control of the situation," I shot back.

Emil's speech began to slur.

I directed my attention to the rest of the pack. "Leave us alone or your leader dies."

The wolves snarled and snapped their powerful jaws.

I concentrated on Emil's blood. I pushed it so that the liquid collected in his upper thigh.

"Do you feel that?" I asked Emil. "That's a clot above your knee. The next stop is your lungs."

Emil paled. "What...kind...of...magic...?"

"Tell your pack to stand down," I urged.

Emil swallowed hard.

I clenched my hands and drew more blood to the site. "Tell them!"

"Stand down," he growled.

The werewolves lowered their heads and backed away so their bottoms were against the far wall. Still too close for comfort but better than nothing.

"Now disperse," I said. I broke apart the clot and released my hold on the werewolf's blood.

A wall of fire dropped down between us and I looked over my shoulder to see George perched on a hole in the wall. The hole seemed just big enough for us to fit through.

We had seconds to escape. As soon as Emil recovered, the wolves would be after us.

I darted to the hole and George moved out of the way to

let me pass. I slid through with no problem. Alaric was a different story. The vampire's shoulders were too broad. Under normal circumstances, I'd make a Winnie the Pooh reference.

But there was no time for jokes.

From the outside I pushed the concrete next to the window in an effort to widen the space. It refused to budge.

The fire continued to block them, but the wolves would simply retreat over the partial wall and run to this side of the building.

"Back away," Alaric commanded.

I hurried a few steps back as pieces of concrete sprayed in all directions. The vampire had punched a large hole next to the window. He climbed through and we took off.

George hovered above us, spewing fire to keep the wolves at bay. I had no idea how they found us. Even with heightened senses, they'd have to know we were in the area in the first place. Questions for a moment of calm. Right now the goal was survival.

We ran blindly through the streets. It wasn't often that Prince Alaric of House August found himself prey instead of predator, whereas I had plenty of experience as both.

The minivan was in the opposite direction. We'd have to find another ride.

Alaric raced to an oversized pickup truck with huge tires parked on the street. With the side of his fist, he smashed open the window to unlock it.

"Get in," he shouted.

I ran to the passenger side. The truck was already in motion. I grabbed the handle on the inside of the door and vaulted into the seat, jamming my knee on the dashboard. I swung the door closed on a wolf snout. The werewolf squealed and slipped away. I closed the door and locked it.

Tires squealed and kicked up dirt as we picked up speed. I twisted to see the wolves growing smaller and smaller. They were fast, but not as fast as this souped-up truck.

I glanced through the windshield to see George flying above us. I slumped against the seat with relief.

Neither of us spoke until the wolves were no longer in view.

"What the hell?" he breathed.

"My sentiments exactly."

My heartbeat slowed and I rested my head against the window. I hadn't gotten enough rest. Soon I'd be too tired to carry on.

"Who leaves their keys in a truck like this?" I asked.

"Didn't you notice the design on the side?"

"Sorry. There wasn't time to admire the detailed craftsmanship."

Alaric smirked. "It says 'Emil's Sweet Ride.'"

I threw my head back and laughed. Served him right.

"You don't think he has tracking on it, do you?"

The vampire shook his head. "Emil strikes me as the kind of guy with a local reputation. I'm guessing nobody within the Baltimore city limits would dare touch his truck."

I shifted my gaze to the passing scenery, which mostly consisted of dilapidated buildings. Lights were few and far between.

"They're part of a resistance group," Alaric said.

"I heard what he said."

"He was there to kill me and free you."

I glanced at him. "I was there, remember?"

He broke into a broad grin. "You like me. You really like me."

I turned away in a huff and forced my gaze outside.

"That's twice now you could've sacrificed me for your freedom. Is this some sort of Stockholm Syndrome?"

"Of course not." I felt my cheeks grow warm and kept my head aimed at the window so he couldn't see.

House Nilsson. Werewolves. Resistance groups.

I remembered Meghan's criticism of me. Maybe she was right. Maybe it was time to do my own research and stop blindly accepting what I'd been told. I was an indentured servant but that didn't prevent me from thinking for myself. I'd grown complacent these past few years. It was time to take back what little control I had of my life.

Alaric's voice cut through my thoughts. "Do you think they're responsible for my father's death? This resistance group?"

I drummed my fingers on the passenger door. "I'm not sure. Either way, how did they know where to find us?"

"It's possible we've had trackers on our tail this whole time. Maybe we lost them for a bit when we took our detour through the Wasteland but now they've caught up to us again."

It was possible.

"Who stands to benefit if House August falls?" I asked.

"Don't overthink it. The wizard might've been lying. House Nilsson has the most to gain. Add our territory to theirs and they'll be the most powerful House in the world."

I reclined my seat, thinking. "There's a treaty. Why violate it now after all this time? What would they have to gain at this moment to force them to act?"

We sat in silence as we each contemplated my question.

Alaric spoke first. "I've got nothing."

"Same. Maybe you're right and Santana was just trying to confuse us." I straightened in my seat. "I have an idea."

The prince looked at me sideways. "Why am I suddenly nervous?"

"Let's go directly to the source."

He grunted. "You want to go to Minneapolis and ask King Stefan if he murdered my father in order to start a House war? That's a helluva detour, Britt."

The seat of House Nilsson was about a thousand miles northwest of our current location.

"I know someone who can get us there fast."

"Of course you do." He exhaled. "Any chance this someone is nearby?"

"As far as I know."

Alaric tapped the steering wheel. "Even if we can get there quickly, we could be walking straight into the lion's den."

"Or we could get answers and stop a war from breaking out."

He fixed me with a lazy grin that warmed me from the inside out. "If you're wrong, my mother will kill you, you know."

"If I'm wrong, we'll already be dead."

His hold on the wheel tightened. "My father would've chosen to fight. That's the kind of king he was."

I looked at him with fresh eyes, this dashing prince with the devil-may-care grin who chose to face monsters with me instead of protecting his own royal ass.

"And which kind of king do you want to be?"

# ELEVEN

It had been about five years since I'd last seen Priscilla Nowak. I met her when I was hired for a last-minute job that involved travel to Nashville where the target was scheduled to appear in public. Michael Burdock had been the leader of a vampire cartel with a long history of criminal activity. He'd finally retired and become a recluse, but one of his enemies kept tabs on him. My client. The client only learned of the Nashville trip the day of and I had to move quickly. Unfortunately I was nowhere near Nashville at the time. The client was willing to spare no expense and arranged for me to meet Priscilla. Portal magic was rare and generally only available to those with cash to spare.

Priscilla lived about fifty miles northwest of Baltimore in what was essentially a luxurious treehouse. Unless you could fly, the only way to reach the entrance was to be invited by Priscilla herself. Door-to-door salespeople and religious zealots didn't stand a chance.

The house consisted of two towers amidst giant bamboo trees connected by a bridge. The building was set about one hundred feet off the ground, which would have afforded

Priscilla panoramic views of the forest and a nearby lake if the countryside weren't bathed in perpetual darkness. There were no windows, just rooms that opened straight to nature.

Alaric parked the truck on the dirt road that led to the treehouse. "Interesting high-rise. Guess she's not too concerned about dragons."

At the mention of dragons, George appeared in front of the windshield. I exited the truck to greet him. "Glad to see you're still with us." I pointed to the treehouse. "Think you could bring Priscilla a message for me?" George wasn't always good with transporting messages. Sometimes they ended up as ashes before they reached their destination.

The pygmy dragon flapped his wings in agreement.

"If my mother had sent a portal witch to Palm Beach, I'd be back in New York safe and sound," Alaric commented.

"Portal witches aren't exactly running rampant. There's a reason Priscilla's services are in high demand."

"She must get special dispensation from our House to use her portal magic. Why not require her to live within the New York border for our convenience?"

I scoffed. "Then she'd simply portal to another territory where those restrictions weren't placed on her. She's good for the economy whether you benefit directly from her services or not. Who do you think pays for the upkeep of all these trees?"

He observed the tall, woody grass. "I didn't know bamboo could grow here."

"It's cheap and easy, just like that vampire you took to the May Day ball."

He winced. "Ooh, a direct hit."

I'd worked security for the event and it had taken all my self-control not to dump a vat of blood on both their heads.

"Bamboo doesn't require as much magic as other plants, which makes it cheaper to sustain."

"We should add bamboo to some of our other properties. Save a few dollars."

As I returned to the truck to hunt for something to write on, a silhouette emerged from inside the treehouse. Even from this distance, I could tell she was stark naked.

"Who's there?" she called.

I averted my gaze. I'd forgotten her preference for nudity. It was one of the reasons she made sure no one could enter her home without warning. She only dressed when she was expecting company and, depending on the company, not even then.

Alaric stared at the treehouse. "Is she...?"

I slapped a hand over his eyes. "Yes." With my hand still in place, I yelled, "Priscilla, it's Britt."

There was a brief pause and then a cheerful voice called, "Death Bringer, is that really you? I thought you died."

I waved. "Nope. Still here."

"How wonderful. I won't be two shakes of a lamb's tail." The figure turned toward the house, giving us a full moon. Only when she disappeared from view did I remove my hand from the prince's eyes.

He looked at me, disgruntled. "What's the big deal? It's nothing I haven't seen before. Everybody has body parts."

Two minutes later Priscilla appeared on the ground in front of us dressed in a gold knit jumpsuit, platform shoes, and dangly earrings. Her red hair was fashioned in a high ponytail. Her makeup was equally dramatic with thick, dark lashes and black eyeliner that extended to her temples.

She hobbled forward and gripped my shoulders. "I can't believe it's you," she said, leaning forward to kiss each cheek.

Not willing to be overlooked, George tapped her ponytail with his wing. She spun around and clapped like a giddy teenager. "George, you delicious creature. I'm so pleased to see you both."

Alaric cleared his throat. The prince wasn't accustomed to being outshone by his companions.

"Priscilla, this is my traveling companion, Colin."

Her smile was quickly replaced by a frown. "Colin? Do I look like a moron to you?" She bowed. "Your Highness, I'm honored to make your acquaintance."

Alaric and I exchanged uneasy glances. Well, at least she knew we could afford her services.

"I understand this is last minute, but we're in need of a portal," Alaric said.

She flicked a dismissive finger. "We can't talk business yet. First Britt the Bloody and I need to have a drink and catch up. You're welcome to join us."

The witch held out her hand, palm raised, and moved it in a circular motion. Energy crackled and a dark hole appeared. She crooked a finger at us and we approached the portal together.

George didn't bother. He simply flew toward the treehouse. I stepped through the dark hole and emerged in Priscilla's living room. The interior was as flamboyant as her outfit. The black, white, and gold color scheme wasn't what anyone expected in a treehouse. Plumes of white feathers three feet in length erupted from a pot on the floor. A black circular sofa took center stage. It was large enough to seat six, although I had no doubt the witch had squeezed more than that on there during one of her outrageous parties. Her style choices seemed incongruous for a woman who preferred the minimalism of nudity. The witch was an enigma.

Priscilla strutted toward the bar. "What's your poison?" She plucked a bottle from the counter. "This red wine is from one of your House vineyards, Your Highness." She wiggled the bottle. "Very pricey, I might add."

"As most wine is," he replied.

Vineyards were expensive to run because of the amount of magic involved to keep the plants alive. It took hundreds of witches and wizards to power them.

She used her teeth to remove the cork and pushed it from her lips with a seductive *pop*. "Will George be joining you?" Priscilla scanned the room. "Where did he go?"

"Hunting. I think he remembers the grand feast he enjoyed the last time we were here." I had no doubt this forest was one of the dragon's favorite places. When I found him in a clearing upon my return from Nashville, he'd been slumped against a tree stump in a happy daze.

"Probably safer if he stays behind," Alaric said. "I don't know their policy on dragons. They might be stricter about pygmies than our House."

Priscilla swilled her wine. "Don't worry, darlings. I'll take good care of him until you get back." She sauntered toward the counter, hips swaying provocatively. "Now if you'll give me the exact location of your destination, I can prep the portal."

"We need you to sign an NDA first," I said.

Priscilla pressed a palm flat against her chest. "Darling Britt, don't you trust me?" She tossed her head back and laughed. "I'm teasing. I've got a template ready." She retrieved a sheet of paper from the drawer of a nearby desk and handed it to me.

"It's standard," I told the prince.

Priscilla pulled a pen from between her boobs and dangled it in front of him. He swiped the pen and signed. Then Priscilla signed, writing her name in large loops.

"Minneapolis," I said. "House Nilsson."

Her eyes widened slightly. "The compound?"

"You can get us inside the compound?" Alaric asked.

She smiled. "I hear the alarm in your voice, Your Highness. Don't worry. I can't breach wards." She inclined her head toward me. "That's Britt the Bloody's job over here."

"She can get us just outside the ward," I said.

Priscilla flipped her ponytail off her shoulder. "I'm very precise."

"How?" the prince asked.

"It's a rare gift. My only gift, actually. I have no other skills." She stopped talking and burst into laughter. "Okay, no magical skills." She held up a finger. "No. That's not true either."

"We get it. Your witchy abilities are portals only." Just like mine was blood. We were both rare witches, except her skill wasn't reviled by most of the population. A portal witch would never have been kicked out of a coven and punished for her uniqueness. She would have been revered.

Alaric still seemed to be processing the information. "And you don't need candles or a spell or a magic circle?"

"This whole house is a magic circle and it's constantly turned on." She licked her lips. "Speaking of which, the three of us would make an appealing sandwich, don't you think? Between our buns and his meat in the middle?" Her eyes flashed with hunger. "Why don't we expend a little energy before you march into battle?"

"We're not marching into battle," I said quickly. "It's a diplomatic visit. Nothing more." Even with the NDA, I didn't need word to get out that the Houses were in secret talks.

Alaric bowed slightly. "As flattered as I am, my mind is focused on more important matters."

I listened in stunned silence. The prince didn't even bother to flirt back. Never in my wildest dreams would I have expected such a polite refusal.

Priscilla's bright red lips formed an exaggerated pout. "Too bad. Maybe on the return journey, once you've taken care of business there, the three of us can take care of business here." She punctuated the suggestion with a wink.

To his credit, Alaric maintained a neutral expression.

"If you're ready then, I'll fire up the portal."

"How will we get back?" the vampire asked.

Priscilla retrieved a bracelet from the pocket of her jumpsuit. "One of you wears this. Press the button when you're ready and it'll notify me to open the portal."

The button was cleverly camouflaged to look like the other black pearls. I slipped the bracelet over my wrist.

"Ready now?" she prompted.

I gave her a thumbs up and she extended her hand, palm up.

Alaric looked at me. "Should we hold hands?"

"Oh, you should definitely hold hands," Priscilla interjected. "Or maybe cup her butt cheek. That works too."

Alaric's hand slid along my waist and came to rest on my ass. He gave it a gentle squeeze as the portal appeared.

I grabbed his hand and held it firmly at his side. His low chuckle morphed into a faint buzz as we stepped through the portal.

Lights blazed and I was forced to shut my eyes as we emerged in Minneapolis. It seemed House Nilsson used bright lights as part of their security system because they stretched as far as I could see. The sprawling building was nearly five million square feet. Before the Eternal Night, the royal compound was known as the Mall of America. Filled with shops, humans would flock here to purchase clothing and household goods and dine at restaurants. That all ended with the Great Eruption. Thanks to its proximity to the calderas that spanned Idaho, Wyoming, Colorado, Utah, and Nevada, the Midwest was hard hit by the wrath of the supervolcanoes. At first even the vampires avoided the states farther west. Once the dust settled, however, the vampires of House Nilsson began staking claims on land and killing anyone who opposed them. The path now known as the Bloody Trail extended all the way from New Orleans to Minneapolis. Although King Stefan wasn't the House founder, he was reportedly every bit as ruthless and bloodthirsty as his predecessors.

Alaric surveyed the massive building. "Where are the guards?"

"Inside, I expect. Between the lights and the ward, they probably feel well-protected out here."

"And who would want to trek all the way to the middle of nowhere to oppose them?"

I suppressed a smile. "Are you seriously playing the superiority card?" There was a long-standing rivalry between the East Coast territories and those in the Midwest. The vampires that lived on the East Coast couldn't understand how any vampire would choose to live in the desolate area owned by House Nilsson. They viewed their Midwest counterparts as less intelligent and less sophisticated.

"What's our plan? You break the ward and we walk in and demand answers?"

My mouth hung open. "That's not a serious suggestion, is it?"

"I think King Stefan will respond to a show of strength."

"And I think his guards will respond to a show of stupidity. We can't show our hand. The second they realize I can break wards, they'll lock me up and throw away the key."

"Fine. Then what do you propose?"

I folded my arms and observed the enormous building. "We wait for them to notice us. They must have security sweeps." I knew the timing of most, if not all, of House August's regular patrols. It wouldn't surprise me to learn House Nilsson had a similar setup.

"Or we could draw their attention to us now and save valuable time." Sharp fangs descended as he grabbed my arm and pulled me close. He thrust back my head, leaving my neck exposed. The points of his fangs traced a line down my neck to my collarbone and an involuntary shudder escaped me. Memories flashed in my mind of the two of us ensconced in his silk sheets, sucking every last ounce of pleasure out of our limited time together.

This was not a good time for reminiscing.

His lips grazed my earlobe. "You'll only feel a pinch."

"I know. Not my first time with you, remember?" I shot back.

His fangs sank into my flesh and I gasped. I'd forgotten how good it felt. How much I missed it.

I felt slightly dizzy as he righted me. "Why will this attract their attention more than breaching the ward or just waving?"

"Oh, it won't. I only wanted to sneak that in case we never get the opportunity again."

I was torn between belting him and letting him do it again.

A voice interrupted our heated moment. "You're on royal grounds. State your business."

I turned to regard a set of vampires. They wore the purple and gold colors of House Nilsson and each carried a gun and a sword in their holsters.

"I'm Prince Alaric of House August and I request an audience with His Majesty, King Stefan, and Her Majesty, Queen Margot."

"House August? You've come a long way." He searched behind us as though our means of transportation might appear. "And who's this?"

"Her name is of no consequence," Alaric barked. "I have important news to share and there's no time to waste."

The guard hesitated. "Fine, but she stays here."

Alaric placed a proprietary hand on my shoulder. "My concubine is not to leave my side. She travels everywhere with me."

I fought the strong desire to punch him in the crotch for that statement.

The gaze of the guards raked over me and the one on the left nodded his approval. "I like blondes, too. Their blood tastes lighter and sweeter."

"I'm more of an acquired taste," I said.

"Come with me." The guard marched toward the compound. Two more sets of guards fell in step on either side of us.

We entered through a set of enormous glass doors. The ceiling was higher than I imagined. I thought there might be complete floors above us, but this section was open all the way to the roof. We passed smaller rooms along the way. They appeared to be barracks for the guards. In New York, House August mainly kept their compound to themselves and we lived in the surrounding buildings. Then again, this former mall was enormous. The king and queen probably needed a guide to find the dining room.

We climbed a set of black steps to the second level. The compound struck me as a different type of maze to the one in the Wasteland. There were too many rooms to count. We passed one room with a long table in the center surrounded by vampires.

"It's the weekly potluck," one of the guards informed us.

"I'm missing out on puppy chow," another complained.

"You should've told Xander to save you some," the first guard said.

"What's puppy chow?" I asked. I didn't know any vampires that ate dog food.

"Oh, you haven't lived until you've tasted puppy chow," the second guard said. "If the king and queen don't kill you, find me after and I'll get you a bag."

"Sounds like a plan," I said.

The guards escorted us to a large room with two thrones on a raised platform. The thrones were surprisingly minimalist. Silver chairs, one with a red butterfly made of gemstones and the other adorned with a dark blue one. The light from the gemstones cast interesting shadows on the walls and floor.

The king and queen filed in a moment later, not bothering to look at us until they were fully seated.

"Prince Alaric, to what do we owe this unexpected pleasure?" King Stefan asked. He didn't *look* particularly ruthless. His light hair was streaked with silver, the sign of a long-lived vampire, but his intimidating qualities ended there. His nose was thin and sharp and his eyes were slightly too close together, giving him a rodent-like appearance.

"The resemblance to your father is uncanny," the queen interrupted. "We are so deeply sorry to hear of his passing."

The word was definitely out.

Alaric bristled. "He didn't 'pass.' He was murdered. Assassinated."

I watched the king and queen closely to gauge their reaction to the news.

The queen clutched her necklace. "Assassinated? By whom?"

"Truthfully, we don't know," Alaric said.

The king frowned. "And you came to us for assistance in this matter?"

Alaric was in a tricky spot. He couldn't accuse them outright without grave consequences. And the fact that they seemed genuinely shocked and hadn't yet tossed us in a dungeon seemed to support the wizard's claim.

The prince seemed to be of the same mindset because he said, "We believe someone is trying to pit our Houses against each other. The information we received pointed a finger at your House, Your Majesty."

The queen pursed her lips. "While there's no love lost between our Houses, I can assure you my husband and I are not involved in an assassination plot, a coup, or anything of the kind. Our attention is currently directed inward." Her lips curved into a smile and I saw that her hand rested on her swollen belly.

Alaric bowed his head. "Congratulations, Your Majesty. That's wonderful news for House Nilsson."

"We thought I'd moved past my child-bearing years, but surprise!" The queen laughed gaily, although I saw a hint of sorrow in her eyes. There was a story there. Maybe she'd been looking forward to her childfree golden years or maybe she'd reluctantly agreed to carry another child to hold the king's interest. Either way, she wasn't entirely happy with the situation.

The king reached over and placed a hand on his wife's arm. "We are delighted, as you can imagine. There's always room for one more in our House."

No kidding. This compound was big enough for a thousand more, although poor Queen Margot didn't seem up for the challenge of single-handedly filling a stadium.

Out of the corner of my eye I glanced at Alaric and noticed his expression. There was a hint of sorrow evident on his face as well. Was he reflecting the queen's emotions or lamenting the loss of his father and, with him, his House's ability to procreate?

It was impossible to tell.

King Stefan seemed to notice me for the first time. "How about you, Alaric? Any plans for fatherhood? I know you're still young, but the sooner you start, the more seeds you can sow."

Inwardly I cringed.

The queen swatted her husband's hand. "Oh, my dear Stefan. Now isn't the time. Besides, you've heard the tales as well as I. The prince has been more interested in sowing wild oats than seeds."

Alaric forced a devil-may-care grin. "Too true, Your Majesty."

"How is your poor mother handling the news?" The queen released a quiet gasp. "My handmaiden recently showed me a lovely photograph of her wearing the most exquisite hat." She shook her head. "Honestly, I don't know how she manages to look so savage and sophisticated at the same time. It's a gift."

Alaric shrugged. "She's a marvel, my mother."

The king pinned Alaric with his beady, rodent eyes. "And which party do you think might be responsible for an attempt to start a war between us?"

"I haven't heard anything at all," the queen interrupted. "I was the one who told the king about your father's death and there was no mention of murder."

"And she keeps tabs on all the gossip, believe me. Those ladies-in-waiting of hers love to chat almost as much as they like to feed." Laughing, King Stefan patted his wife's knee. The look on his wife's face suggested she might do the same—except much harder.

"We would appreciate any help you can offer," Alaric said.

"I'll speak to my advisors immediately," King Stefan said. "In the meantime, you must stay and rest."

"You look in desperate need of a shower," Queen Margot added. "We'll have a room prepared for you and your companion."

I stiffened.

"I appreciate the generous offer, Your Majesty, but it's important I continue my search for the guilty parties," Alaric replied.

The king's eyes narrowed dangerously. "You would refuse my hospitality?"

"Let us dine together and discuss the matter at greater length," the queen interjected. "My husband will bring news from his advisors."

I had a feeling she had experience soothing the savage beast beside her. I almost felt sorry for her, except for the fact that she was a vampire queen. I'd never managed to muster up enough empathy to feel sorry for vampires.

The guards escorted us to a room where two ladies-in-waiting were scurrying around like mice, giving the place a last polish. I noticed two sets of clean towels folded on the bench at the end of the bed. A shower *would* be good. A nap would be better.

Alaric snatched the first set of towels and blew me a kiss as he disappeared into the bathroom.

"Scoundrel!" I called after him. I debated calling Liam with an update but decided to wait. If House Nilsson was anything like House August, they had listening devices installed in their guest rooms.

Before I could rest my weary head, the queen appeared in the doorway and snapped her fingers. The ladies-in-waiting filed out of the room, leaving me alone with the queen.

"Where is the prince?"

"From the sound of the water, I'd say he's already in the shower."

The queen brushed past me. "Who are you?" she asked, her voice as gentle as it was in the throne room.

"I'm the mistress of His Highness."

"Nonsense. Look at you. You're no more the prince's concubine than I'm ready to be a doting mother yet again."

Well, it seemed we'd both pegged each other correctly.

I saw no reason to lie at this point. "My name is Britt. I'm an indentured servant of House August."

"Tell me, Britt. Does House August typically send their indentured servants along on diplomatic missions?"

"I wouldn't know what's typical of House August decisions, Your Majesty."

She assessed me fully. "One of the guards recognized you. He says you're an assassin called Death Bringer." Her hands rested on her burgeoning belly. "Are you here to murder us?"

"No, Your Majesty. We're here for the reason the prince said—to find out who murdered King Maxwell and why your Houses are being pitted against each other. Someone wants House August to believe you're to blame and Queen Dionne is buying the lie hook, line and sinker."

A handmaiden hurried into the room. "Your Majesty, an urgent message has arrived. Should we bring it to the king?"

"You know better than that, Joyce." The queen wiggled her fingers. "Bring it here."

Joyce faltered. "Are you sure, Your Majesty? In here? You might want to come to the throne room to receive this one."

"Nonsense. If it's urgent, I'm not about to run there. You know what the healer said."

Joyce lowered her head. "As you wish, Your Majesty."

My throat ran dry as I waited for the message to reveal itself.

The handmaiden returned accompanied by two guards. One of the guards held the head of a vampire on a spike.

The queen recoiled. "Is that our scout?"

The guard clutching the spike nodded. "Arrived by butterfly horde an hour ago."

The mouth opened and the head began to talk. "We have incontrovertible evidence that you, House Nilsson, have breached the treaty with House August in an attempt to overthrow our rule and seize our lands. As such, in accordance with paragraph B(3)(c), we are declaring war upon your House."

My heart pounded. What evidence? There was no evidence.

"Take the head away and burn it," the queen commanded. "Do not mention this to the king. Not yet."

The guards retreated with the messenger along with the handmaiden.

The queen turned her gaze to me and I fought to remain calm. No doubt she believed Alaric and I were here to slay them from the inside, especially now that she knew my identity. My fingers itched to retrieve my blade, but I resisted. I didn't want to make any move that might provoke her.

Finally the queen spoke. "It seems you and your prince were right all along, Death Bringer. Someone is determined to bring down both our Houses in one go."

It took a moment for her words to register. "You believe us?"

"I do now." She sat on the bed and patted beside her. "Tell me everything, my dear, including the details of your relationship with the handsome prince if there's time."

I heard the shower water turn off. "There definitely isn't time for that, Your Majesty."

I debated how much information to divulge. Under the circumstances, it seemed best to be forthcoming. House August troops were on the way and we needed House Nilsson not to overreact. That meant winning them over with whatever tool I had at my disposal. Right now that tool was honesty.

"Once the queen learned of her husband's murder, she sent me to retrieve the prince and deliver him safely to New York. She worried that Prince Alaric was a target, too."

"But why blame us?"

"Because you're the obvious choice. We want the truth, which is the reason we decided to take the risk and come directly to you. Something must've happened in New York to convince the queen of your guilt. When I left, she was more than willing to wait for Alaric to make a move."

A vague smiled passed her lips. "Dionne never was suited to the throne. A beautiful vampire. Fearless in fashion, but not so much in House matters. I suppose she intends to pass the crown directly to Alaric. I would do the same in her position."

Another handmaiden appeared in the doorway, wringing her hands.

The queen regarded her. "What is it, girl?"

The servant's gaze darted from the queen to me. "There's something you should know, Your Majesty."

The queen rolled her hand. "Go on then. Out with it."

"You remember how you gave me permission to visit my gran in Chicago?"

"That explains why I didn't recognize her," the queen muttered to me. She directed a blinding smile at the servant. "And how long were you away?"

"Three weeks. Got back yesterday, Your Majesty."

"And we couldn't have done without you for another day. Welcome back. How's your nan?"

"My gran. She died, Your Majesty."

The queen puckered her lips in a display of sympathy. "Such a shame. The circle of life can be such a beast." She turned toward me to resume our conversation.

"I...I wasn't finished, Your Majesty," the servant interrupted.

Queen Margot swiveled toward her. "Yes?"

"Between here and Chicago, I saw things." The servant swallowed. "I wasn't sure what to make of it then, but listening to you now..." Her cheeks flamed. "Not that I was eavesdropping, Your Majesty."

The queen groaned. "Spit it out, girl, or I'll have silver hair by the time you've finished."

"I saw vampire camps."

The queen frowned. "What do you mean by camps? Describe them for me."

The servant lowered her head and spoke in a soft voice. "Like caravans of vampires."

It was my turn to ask the girl a question. "How many miles from here would you say they are?"

The servant silently counted on her fingers. "Two hundred miles, give or take, miss."

Two hundred miles didn't give us much time.

The queen's elegant fingers gripped the bedspread.

"Even with their fastest vampires at the front, I don't think House August could've moved that quickly," I said. And nobody possessed the magical energy required to create a portal suitable for an entire army. Whoever these vampires were, I didn't think they were acting on behalf of House August.

Queen Margot rose to pace the floor. "A lesser House attempting a comeback?"

"Possibly."

The queen seemed to remember the handmaiden was still there. "Thank you, girl."

"It's Gilly, Your Majesty."

"Thank you, Gilly. Go to the kitchen now and tell Myra to give you one of our Blue Ribbon bottles of blood."

Gilly lit up like she'd been handed the keys to the kingdom. She scurried from the room before the queen could change her mind.

Queen Margot gave me her full attention now. "What do you suggest we do, Death Bringer?"

"Me?"

"Our emotions will be running hot, but yours, I imagine, will remain cool and collected. A necessity in your line of work, one would think."

It was. "I think we should tell your husband and Prince Alaric."

"Naturally, but I'd still like to hear your thoughts first because they're clouded by the opinions of men."

I opened my mouth to defend Alaric, but quickly thought better of it. Truth be told, I understood what she meant.

"If I were you, I would send scouts—a joint party—to figure out who they are and what their intentions are."

"I have two of the fastest scouts in the region right here in the compound," she said. "I'll send Lindberg."

"A portal would be better. Do you have a witch on staff?"

The queen scowled. "Not anymore and we haven't replaced her yet."

I didn't dare ask what happened to her, but my intuition told me it had something to do with King Stefan's wandering body parts.

"I might be able to help with that."

The queen arched a thin eyebrow. "You possess portal magic?"

"No, but I know someone who does."

The queen closed her eyes for a brief moment, as though mentally preparing herself for next steps. Finally she looked at me and said with a trace of bitterness, "It's time to share this update with the king."

# TWELVE

King Stefan stared at us with a blank expression. The news about the approaching army didn't seem to rattle him as much as I anticipated.

Alaric, on the other hand, looked downright baffled. "I swear to you, Your Majesty, I can't imagine my mother acting this swiftly, certainly not without my input."

"But you are here and not there." The king eyed him with suspicion. "I am beginning to think your unexpected visit was a ruse after all."

Alaric clenched his hands into fists. "And I give you my word that it isn't the case. I came here in good faith."

"Then perhaps your mother is more cunning than you give her credit for."

I could see the king's paranoia rising to the surface and spilling into the throne room. We had to figure out a way to convince him or we might find ourselves on the wrong side of a prison door, or worse.

"Husband, consider the facts," Queen Margot entreated. "What reason would they have for coming here? If they intended to attack, they would've done so already."

Alaric's eyebrows inched up in response to the queen's intervention on our behalf.

"Not if they wanted someone on the inside to open the doors," the king countered.

We didn't have time to coddle him. The clock was ticking. "I would've killed you both, Your Majesty, and Alaric would've opened the doors for his House. We'd have no need to keep you alive."

King Stefan drew to his full height. "Do you dare suggest you could overpower me?"

The queen backhanded his arm. "Pipe down, husband. We both know you have a bad back and a bum knee. Besides, she's the assassin known as Death Bringer. She wouldn't even need to touch you to kill you where you stand."

The king regarded me skeptically. "Never heard of her."

The queen ushered him aside. "One of these days, my king, you will learn that women of all species are multi-talented creatures." She flicked a glance at Alaric. "We'll send a scout to verify the identity of the interlopers."

"Good plan," the prince replied.

"It was hers," she said, inclining her head toward me. "She knows a portal witch who can send the scout. She recommended a joint party and I agree. They're only two hundred miles away so time is of the essence."

King Stefan's jaw clicked open and shut. "Have I mentioned how much I love it when you take charge?"

The queen rubbed her belly. "I believe the last time you told me was six months ago, dearest."

The king cast a fond look at his wife before releasing a shrill whistle. Three guards entered the room in unison.

"I need Lindberg," he thundered. "Now!"

The guards practically knocked each other over in their effort to escape the throne room in search of Lindberg.

"He'll come with us," Alaric said.

King Stefan clutched his sides and bellowed. "Do you really think I'm foolish enough to send my best scout with the two of you to investigate?"

The queen's face grew flushed. "You'll have to forgive my husband. He's incapable of singing more than one note."

Alaric's shoulders tensed and I sensed he was about to say something I might regret. "Then Britt will accompany him. I'll stay here as your guest or your prisoner. You decide."

The prince was laying it all on the line to persuade the king to trust us. It was a bold and terrifying move.

I removed my phone from my pocket. "He'll even call the queen and try to persuade her."

"She'll think I'm holding him prisoner. That the call is a threat." King Stefan tapped his ring on the arm of the throne. The click echoed throughout the room. "Very well then," he finally said. "The prince stays. You may go."

A lone vampire rushed into the room and immediately dropped to bended knee. "You summoned me, Your Majesty."

"Rise, Lindberg. I have a task for you." The king motioned me forward. "This will be your companion."

"Nice to meet you, Lindberg. Now hold my hand." I wiggled my fingers and the vampire reluctantly grasped them. Then I initiated the trigger on the black pearl bracelet.

A black hole formed. We entered the portal and arrived in the living room of the treehouse. Poor Lindberg fell to his knees and vomited.

Priscilla stared at the mess on the floor. "What the hell? You brought me a virgin?"

"Sorry about that," the vampire said and rose to his feet.

"Swapping partners already?" Priscilla gave him a long look. "Not as handsome or muscular, but I suppose he'll do."

Lindberg looked ready to melt into the puddle that was already on the floor.

"She's our ticket to ride," I explained.

Priscilla clapped her hands together. "Oh, I like that description."

"We need a portal to take us two hundred miles east of Minneapolis on the same route as Chicago," I told her. "And the ability to be whisked straight back again."

Priscilla tightened her ponytail. "I don't have plans today so works for me."

Lindberg glanced around the treehouse in awe. "What is this place?"

"Welcome to my not-so-humble abode," Priscilla said, shifting her hips. "Do you like what you see?"

The vampire's gaze lingered on our hostess. "Very much so."

Priscilla pivoted to me. "Well, there's nothing wrong with his eyesight."

"I should hope not. He's a scout."

Her eyes sparkled. "Ooh, what are we scouting?"

"Never mind." I linked arms with my companion. "Can we get a move on? It's rather urgent."

She rolled her eyes. "Well, if it's *rather* urgent..."

The portal appeared and I dragged Lindberg through with me. "No vomiting this time, please."

He belched. "No promises."

The portal thrust us forward into an open field.

Lindberg's eyes skated to me. "Who are you anyway?"

"A witch."

"No, I mean, why are you involved?"

"I work for House August."

"As what?"

"Doesn't matter. What matters is figuring out who's heading toward Minneapolis because I can tell you right now, it isn't House August."

He shrugged. "If you say so."

"I mean it. House August isn't your enemy."

Lindberg grunted. "I don't know what you've been drinking, but House August is always our enemy."

We emerged from the field and walked along the side of a highway. The land was flat and empty as far as the eye could see.

"Your friend might've aimed her portal a little better," he remarked.

"Everyone's a critic."

A truck whizzed past us without slowing down, spewing a cloud of dust in its wake. I wasn't even sure the driver noticed us.

"Now what?" Lindberg asked. "We walk aimlessly until we stumble upon the enemy camp?"

I was going to stumble across his face in a minute if he didn't rein in the attitude.

"Your friend is pretty hot. Is she seeing anyone?"

I stared at him. "We're in the middle of a dangerous mission and you're thinking about getting set up on a date?"

He grinned. "What can I say? It's been a little while."

I figured I might as well dig for information while I had a willing captive. "What happened to the royal portal witch?"

"Cecily? She left."

"Yes, I got that much. Why?"

Lindberg turned away from me to survey the opposite field. "She got pregnant the same time as the queen. Her Majesty couldn't bear the sight of the witch's growing belly and dismissed her."

"How many children does the king have?"

Lindberg snickered. "No one knows for sure, not even the king himself. Some joke that he's trying to give birth to his own army." The vampire shot me a quick look. "Not me, of course. Wouldn't dream of joking about the king."

I was starting to understand Queen Margot.

I spotted a row of caravans on the horizon. It reminded me of the setup for a traveling carnival.

"It's not House August."

Lindberg squinted. "How can you tell all the way from here?"

"Because Queen Dionne would never approve of those tacky caravans." There was no sign of insignias or family crests. No banners. If a lesser House was making a move, they weren't flaunting it.

Lindberg darted forward and took refuge behind a disused telephone pole. His slender frame was likely one of the reasons he made a good scout. It quickly became apparent that he had no intention of waiting for me. Since he needed me for the return journey, I wasn't sure what he hoped to gain by ditching me.

Subconsciously my finger moved to brush the black pearls around my wrist but I felt only skin. I glanced down and saw that the bracelet was gone. No wonder Lindberg felt fine about leaving me in the dust, that petty thief.

I chased after him as he vacated the pole and edged closer to the row of caravans.

"You're not leaving here without me," I hissed.

He glared at me and put a finger to his lips. I tried to snatch the bracelet off his wrist, but he grabbed my hand and squeezed.

"I'm in charge now."

For a beanpole, the vampire had a ridiculously strong grip. The sound of footsteps forced us to abandon our fight. Lindberg released me and crouched low to the ground.

"Our salvation is at hand. Roma promised," a voice declared.

Who was Roma?

Lindberg had the same reaction because he looked at me with a quizzical expression and mouthed the word 'Roma.'

I ran through the first names of all the lesser Houses, but there was no Roma. They were clearly vampires, albeit a little worse for wear, so a resistance group was out of the question.

"I need a closer look," I whispered. If I could see them more clearly, I might glean helpful information. A color guard. A flag. Anything to help identify the enemy.

I waited for the voices to fade before advancing. I slipped between the metal hook of two caravans. The caravans were part of a larger circle and in the middle was open space where dozens of vampires gathered. Their clothing was different from other vampires I knew. They wore more primitive attire that looked hand-sewn by someone's grandma. Someone's pretty untalented grandma.

"This isn't an army," Lindberg said. "These are wannabe vampires."

"What's a wannabe vampire?"

Lindberg wrinkled his nose in disgust. "The Pey. They're like the lesser version of us. Your intel is bad. They're not coming to fight us. They're scavengers."

The Pey. The name lit up in my mind like a Times Square billboard. We weren't spying on a lesser House or a resistance group.

We were looking at the Angels of Mercy.

Suddenly everything made sense. The unusual skirmishes between packs that left only bones. The Pey were passing through towns like ghosts and leaving carnage in their wake. Even the trail fit. New Jersey. A surreptitious stop in Pittsburgh to assassinate King Maxwell. Toledo. They'd been making their way west to claim their seat at the table.

The reason for the assassination *was* to start a war—but not for power.

For food.

And we were to be their meal ticket.

I ducked lower as two subvampires walked past us, a little too close for comfort. Their senses weren't nearly as heightened as other vampires I knew. Alaric would've known someone was watching, whereas these two subvampires seemed oblivious.

Lindberg inched closer to me. "What now?"

"We need to get back and tell them."

"Tell them what? It's all a big misunderstanding? Like I said, these guys are scavengers. They travel all over the continent in search of scraps."

I held out my hand. "Give me back the bracelet and I'll explain what's happening."

"Nothing's happening. Somebody mistook this caravan for a war party. End of story."

"It's much more than that. Give me back the bracelet. We need to get back and report this."

Hesitation flickered in the vampire's eyes.

"What's your plan?" I demanded. "Leave me here and

tell them something happened to me? You'd have to kill me if you don't expect me to show up with the truth and I don't think you've got the stones for it." He was a scout for a reason.

Lindberg's mouth turned down at the corners. "Is it true about you? That you killed all those vampires?"

Once again my past was coming back to haunt me. I should've guessed.

"The important thing to know is that vampires were my main source of employment. They're the ones who hired me to kill other vampires. It wasn't a vendetta against your species. It was the job I did to survive."

Lindberg's fingers tightened around the bracelet. I didn't want to hurt him, but if it was the choice between getting stuck here and getting back to Alaric, I knew what I was willing to do.

"How is it you're so good at killing us?"

"Because I can do it without even touching you. I can crouch right here across from you and kill you, take back the bracelet, and be on my merry way."

"Then why haven't you?" he challenged.

Lindberg was wasting valuable time. "Because I'm not that person anymore." Most of the time. "How about this? Give me the bracelet and I'll put in a good word for you with Priscilla."

He immediately perked up. "That's the portal witch?"

I nodded. "Did I mention she's a nudist?"

Lindberg only hesitated a split second before he ripped the bracelet off his wrist and passed it to me. I grabbed his hand and triggered the portal.

## THIRTEEN

Lindberg and I went straight from Priscilla's to the House Nilsson compound. To his credit, the vampire didn't vomit again and I managed to pass his number to the portal witch. Whether she used it was up to her. There was no sign of George, but I wasn't concerned. The pygmy dragon always knew how to find me. He was like a colorful, fire-breathing homing pigeon.

The king and queen were dining with Alaric when we arrived, so we were ushered into the dining room.

My stomach gurgled at the sight of so much food. Queen Margot must've noticed my hungry gaze because she insisted we sit and eat while we delivered our report.

Lindberg practically salivated at the bottle of blood on the table and the queen instructed one of the members of staff to pour him a goblet. For a queen, she was impressively attentive to others' needs.

"What do you know about the Pey?" I asked, once I'd downed a glass of water and swallowed a few bites of whatever meat was on the plate. I was too hungry to bother to ask.

"The Pey as in the Angels of Mercy?" the king asked, seemingly perplexed.

"One and the same." I stabbed a carrot spear with my fork and crunched the end.

"They're no threat to us," Lindberg volunteered. "They douse their arrows and spears in poison and use them to finish off their victims and end their suffering."

"End their suffering—or is it so the Pey can enjoy a meal without interruption?" the queen asked.

"You speak as someone with experience," Alaric remarked.

"I have more children than I care to admit, Your Highness," she replied. "An uninterrupted meal is my idea of nirvana."

King Stefan scowled with disdain. "These creatures aren't true vampires. They possess no magic. Why is this a discussion? As Lindberg said, I can simply send our soldiers to their camp and destroy them."

"Except the House August soldiers won't be far behind," Alaric said. "To ask the soldiers to fight again so soon..."

"By then, you will have explained the situation to your mother and the war will be over before it's begun." The king picked up a goblet of blood and drank. Case closed.

"It's not that simple, Your Majesty," Alaric said. "Have you ever tried to stop a tidal wave when it's close to shore? It's gained too much power and momentum by then. If you try to stand your ground and stop it, it'll smash right over you."

The king set down his goblet and glared at the prince. "Are you telling me you can't control your own army? If that's the case, House August has bigger problems than us."

"Now that we know what's really happening," I interrupted, "we can tell Queen Dionne. Let her deal with the army while we deal with the Pey."

Queen Margot raised a goblet to toast me. "An excellent idea."

"If the situation calls for it, how many soldiers can you spare for the Pey?" Alaric asked.

The king grunted. "As many as it takes, although I doubt we need more than a handful."

I worried that they were underestimating what the Pey were capable of. "You may view them as a lower form of vampire, Your Majesty, but they've survived as long as your species, if not longer. They've also managed to assassinate a king without leaving evidence and manipulate two main Houses. I wouldn't treat them as a lesser threat."

Queen Margot regarded me from beneath thick lashes. "The Pey are ruled by a woman. I wouldn't dream of treating them as a lesser threat." She turned to face her husband. "Wouldn't you agree, darling?"

The king seemed to recognize the need to change tack. "Yes, absolutely. Without question."

Lindberg rubbed the back of his neck. "If the Pey don't plan to attack us, then why have they positioned themselves in harm's way?"

"Because they're anticipating the arrival of our soldiers," Alaric explained. "They need to be where the action is so they can reap the rewards."

Lindberg grimaced. "I see." He gulped the remainder of the blood in his goblet. "The Pey are disgusting, if you don't mind me saying, Your Majesty."

I eyed the drips of blood clinging to his lip. "I agree. Disgusting."

"Then it's settled," Queen Margot said. "Call your

mother and tell her what we've learned. She'll call off the soldiers and we'll handle the Pey. Crisis averted."

I finished the last piece of food on my plate, grateful for the chance to refuel. "Is my room still available, Your Majesty?"

"It is," the queen replied. "If you need anything, just ring for one of the ladies."

"Thank you. If you'll excuse me." I was long overdue for a shower. I figured I had enough time to scrub the dirt and blood from the crevices while Alaric dealt with his mother.

When I emerged from the shower fifteen minutes later, Alaric sat on the bench at the foot of the bed with his head in his hands. I wanted to be annoyed that he'd invaded my space when I had only a towel around me, but his posture suggested his mind was on more important matters.

He lifted his head when he heard me approach. "My mother isn't herself."

"What happened?" I joined him on the bench.

"She says the Pey can't possibly be to blame, that House Nilsson has brainwashed me into believing them."

"Did she say why she's convinced they killed your father? What's the smoking gun?"

"Witnesses claim they saw a purple and gold standard in the vicinity when my father was killed."

I balked. "That's it? Somebody spotted two colors associated with House Nilsson and that means they're the guilty party?"

He shook his head. "I know. It's absolute lunacy. She won't listen to reason. I know it's her grief talking, but still."

Queen Dionne was in a downward spiral and she was going to take two Houses with her in the process. At least she knew herself well enough to realize she wasn't fit to rule. If only she'd realize she should listen to her son.

Alaric drew breath. "She'll snap out of it. She has to."

"We don't have time to wait for her to come to her senses, Alaric. Lives are at stake. Do you think the soldiers will listen to you if you try to stop them from advancing?" House August would owe Priscilla a mint, but it was a small price to pay to avoid a war.

Alaric wore a pained expression. "They've never viewed me as a leader, which is entirely my fault, I realize. I don't know that they'll start now, not in the face of conflicting orders from their queen."

"They certainly won't listen to me. I'm the inferior race, remember?" As the statement passed my lips, an unpleasant memory flashed in my mind.

Alaric zeroed in on my expression. "What's wrong? You look ready to assassinate me."

I cleared the painful thoughts from my head. "Nothing. It just slipped out."

"Your face suggests it's a lot more than nothing. Why would you refer to yourself as an inferior race?"

Fine. He wanted to know. I'd toss that truth grenade and see where it landed. "It's from that day at the vineyard."

It took a moment for the words to register. "The vineyard?"

"Yes. You were supposed to meet me there, but you ditched me. Remember?" It was strange how a single word could trigger an avalanche of unwanted memories. I'd spent days on the road with Alaric and managed to keep the past where it belonged, but one wrong word parked all the baggage at the forefront.

"It wasn't a proud moment for me," he admitted.

I half laughed. "If it wasn't a proud moment for you, imagine what it was like for me."

Alaric had promised to take me somewhere outside of

the city so that we could act like a normal couple for a weekend and not hide the relationship. We'd settled on one of the royal vineyards in the Hamptons. He arranged transportation for me and even bought me a dress. I was thrilled. As tough as I'd become, part of me embraced the idea of Cinderella. To shed my 'unclean' skin and emerge as a beautiful princess. I viewed Alaric as both my fairy godmother and my prince rolled into one.

I'd arrived at the vineyard feeling the most excited I'd ever been. As I changed into the dress and fixed my hair, a little voice inside me said that everything would change after this. Alaric would see me with fresh eyes and realize he didn't want to be with anyone else ever again. I'd been young and foolish, I knew that now, but I'd believed it all the same.

When I arrived at the designated spot, Alaric was there —but with another woman, a vampire I recognized from working security at royal events. Her name was Rebecca. He was so engrossed in conversation with her that he didn't notice me approach.

"I heard you've been seen around the city with one of your servants." She'd clucked her tongue in disapproval.

"I have no idea who you mean."

She'd swatted his arm in a playful manner. "Come now, Alaric. We all play with our food on occasion. Just don't forget who you are, Your Highness. Dalliances like that can break a House if you're not careful."

He'd snaked his arm around her waist and the gesture made my blood boil. "It's only a bit of fun, Bex. You know me."

"When the time comes to settle down, you do realize a vampire is your only option," Bex had told him. "There's no point in breeding with someone from an inferior race, no matter how impressive her skills are."

"Why would I ever settle down?" he'd replied and nuzzled her neck.

The memory still burned.

I looked at the prince. "For a brief, shining moment in my life, you made me feel special. Then you took it away in a single moment."

"What are you talking about? You didn't need me for that. You're a rare blood witch. You were already special."

"That's not special. That's an aberration."

He studied me with a mixture of confusion and pain. "I wish you didn't see yourself that way."

I stared at my lap. "You asked me before about my last name."

"You don't have one."

"Not now, but I did when I was younger. It was Miller."

"Yes, I can see why you ditched it. Doesn't suit you. Too plain."

I snorted. "I didn't stop using it because I was too fancy for it. I stopped using it because I wanted to sever the last connection to my parents."

"Britt Miller," he said, testing the name on his tongue. "Nope. Britt the Bloody is much better."

I wasn't sure 'better' was the right word. Both names came with baggage I wanted to unload.

"Nobody wakes up and thinks, *hey, why not become an assassin?*"

"You did what you had to in order to survive. I would never hold that against you."

I shook my head. "There were other options. Options that didn't involve death and destruction. I chose the one that fed the coven's belief that I was a bad seed."

Alaric nudged me. "I think it's normal to behave in a way that's a reaction to our parents' expectations. Look at me. Do you think I'd have been boozing it up in Palm Beach if my father had been a kind and gentle soul? I would've wanted to emulate him instead of—" He waved a hand. "Whatever I've become."

"You were a natural in the Wasteland. I never pictured you fighting like that."

"Because I never wanted to. I knew I had it in me, but I suppressed it because I didn't want to become like my father."

I knew it was more than a reaction for me. The day the coven cast me out, a dark belief had taken root in my soul and flourished there. Alaric's rejection seemed only to confirm that belief. My mother once described love as a shield designed to protect us from harm, or at least buffer the blows of an uncaring world. Later I made the unfortunate discovery that it could be wielded as a sword too.

"To be honest, I didn't start working as an assassin purely to survive. I knew I had a skill that few others possessed and I opted to leverage it. In my own twisted way, I thought I could earn the love and respect of others by becoming the 'best' assassin and gaining an esteemed reputation among my 'betters.'"

"Us," he whispered.

And I'd continued my desperate bid for approval when I became a member of the security team for House August, which was how I ended up seated on a bench with Prince Alaric contemplating our fates.

"I know I should've said this a long time ago, but I'm sorry for what I did to you. How much I hurt you. It was wrong and I knew it was wrong even then, but I was so committed to playing a particular role that I couldn't bring myself to behave better. For what it's worth, I regret my actions. Deeply."

I didn't realize how much I needed to hear that until this moment. A rush of air escaped my lungs. "Thank you for saying that."

"I always thought you were too smart to fall for my act. Do you think that's the reason you got involved with me back then? Another form of approval?"

I hadn't considered that option. "I don't know. Maybe." It was a lot to unpack and right now I had too much on my mind to do the suggestion justice.

"Too bad you weren't able to go on assassinating vampires. Might've been cathartic for you, picturing them all as me."

I squeezed my eyes closed. The joke landed a little too close to home.

"Do you know how I ended up as an indentured servant for your House?" I hadn't told him during our brief relationship. It was a moment I kept to myself, because of the pain it induced and also because of the shame I felt whenever I remembered that day at the market.

"I haven't been privy to those sorts of details." His eyes turned downcast. "I suppose I didn't much care either."

"I used magic outside the scope of my contract."

"That was my assumption."

"I'd accepted a job in Philadelphia for a lower royal in your House. He was settling a debt." Royal vampires were above the law when it came to assassination. There might be a war fought over it, but there would never be a murder trial.

He wore a grim smile. "Let me guess. Cousin Felix. He's always been a vindictive jackass."

"Doesn't matter who. The point is, as I passed by a market, I recognized two witches from Lancaster."

He frowned. "Recognized them from what?"

"Where I'm from. My home." I wrapped my arms around my knees. "They tossed me out like yesterday's trash and the two witches I saw had been front and center when they exiled me. One even spit on me for possessing 'dirty magic.' The second I saw them, that moment came rushing back to me."

Alaric released a quiet breath. "You snapped."

I nodded. "I attacked them instead of my target. I came close to killing them right there in the market."

My behavior that day convinced me that what they believed was true. That I deserved to be cast out. When I chose servitude over death, it wasn't because I was afraid to die. It was because deep down I felt I deserved to suffer. Death would have allowed me to escape real punishment.

Alaric studied me. "How did I not know any of this?"

I didn't hold his ignorance against him. "We didn't do a lot of talking back then."

Silence settled between us. I couldn't bring myself to look at him, to see the revulsion or disappointment.

"One bad decision doesn't tell our whole story," he finally said.

I cocked an eyebrow. "You sure about that?"

"You were a professional killer, yet you didn't kill them. What stopped you?"

I brought my knees to my chest, careful to keep my towel in place. "My parents. If they were alive and learned what I'd done...I couldn't bear the thought." Even though they'd stood by and watched the coven expel me, I still yearned for their love and approval. It was so deeply ingrained in me, I could empty all the blood in my veins and not be rid of the desire. It was a weakness I hated, yet it had saved me from myself that day in the market.

"You've had no contact with your parents since you left Lancaster?"

"Not a peep. Communication was expressly forbidden. It didn't matter. My parents were the ones who told the coven what I could do. They were the reason I was exiled and they did nothing to stop it."

"Seems like we were both dealt the flawed parent card."

I rested my chin on the tops of my knees. "The queen?"

"My mother is too tender to be royal. My father, on the other hand..." He leaned his elbows on the bed and exhaled. "My father was a tenderizer."

"Why did he choose to marry her? I would've thought the strength of the House would trump everything else."

A faint smile touched his lips. "You've seen her. My mother is a beauty. My father couldn't resist her." His smile faded. "Then again, he rarely resisted a beautiful woman."

"But he married *her*. There must've been a reason."

Alaric tipped his head back and stared at the canopy above our heads. "I assume so, but I don't know what it was. He'd originally pledged to marry a princess to form an alliance with House Langley."

House Langley didn't even exist anymore. House August stamped out the former royal vampire line before I was born.

"Do you know why I was in Palm Beach?" he asked.

"The food, the women, the open space?"

"No. My father sent me. He decided I wasn't fit to rule anywhere except the Southern Territories because they're the easiest to control."

"I prefer your exile to mine."

Alaric missed the joke. "I think he resented me for...being me."

And then it hit me. There had been an older brother, Prince Theo, who died during the House's takeover of Boston. House Langley was snuffed out and the territory annexed, but not without great cost to House August.

"You weren't there, were you?" Alaric couldn't have been old enough to fight.

"No, I was too young. I stayed at the compound with my mother. When my father returned, he looked at me with fresh eyes and made it clear to everyone he didn't like what he saw."

"I'm so sorry, Alaric."

"If you could go back to that day at the market, would you handle it differently?" he asked.

"I don't know," I said truthfully. As much shame and guilt as I felt, I didn't think I had more to offer than death. Death Bringer. Britt the Bloody. Death had defined me my entire adult life.

Alaric seemed to sense my thoughts because he said, "You saved those children in the Wasteland. You could've stayed the course and not taken that detour, but you did."

"But I had to kill a lot of monsters along the way." I was still leaving death and destruction in my wake.

"You didn't do it for money or power or any selfish reason. You did it so that someone else might live. Lots of small someone elses."

"You did, too, you know. You could've been selfish and kept going straight to New York."

"Not without my knight protector. I would've been too vulnerable."

Our gazes met and heat rippled through me. "I don't equate Prince Alaric of House August with vulnerability."

His gaze softened. "I take after my mother." He paused. "In looks."

I couldn't resist a smile. "You are a remarkable beauty. Everybody in New York says so."

"Everybody in New York would be right."

His face seemed to move forward in slow motion. His lips hovered mere inches from mine. We stared at each other, each one waiting for the other to make the first move. Heart thumping, I held my breath.

A knock at the door interrupted us.

We sprang apart, relinquishing the moment. I gathered my wits and tried to normalize my breathing.

"Come in," Alaric said.

The queen poked her head inside. "I'm sorry to interrupt. I'm wondering if there's any news."

"You're not interrupting anything," Alaric said.

Of course not. How could I have expected this moment to mean something to him? We'd only shared our innermost secrets.

I was relieved I hadn't kissed him. He'd played me once before. I couldn't let myself fall victim to him again.

"My husband grows impatient. I told him I'd check with you."

"That's my cue to get dressed." I streaked into the bathroom with my clothes tucked under my arm. When I returned to the bedroom, the queen and prince were gone.

I took the opportunity to make a quick call to Liam to update him on the situation.

"Did you give in and bone him yet?" the werewolf asked once we'd finished the serious topic.

I hung up.

I arrived in the throne room in time to catch the tail end

of the discussion. Based on their sober expressions, Alaric had explained the unfortunate situation.

"Then it's war?" the queen asked.

"Not if I can help it. Britt and I will parley with the Pey first and see if we can persuade Roma to turn herself over to our House."

"And if she won't?" the king asked.

"Then we'll need backup."

"I'll send you in my fastest fleet," the king said. "My troops will follow behind you."

"In the meantime, do you have any weapons you can spare?" Alaric asked. "I'm afraid we've come unprepared."

"It seems you are your father's son after all," King Stefan said. His eyes glinted with admiration. "I think it best if I remain here in case the battle rages west, but as a show of good faith, I'll send my two eldest children with you to parley on our behalf. They're skilled in combat and have a hunger for violence should the need arise."

Oh, yippee. Now we were babysitting royal homicidal maniacs on top of everything else.

The king released his trademark shrill whistle. "Send Michael and Genevieve to the armory."

The queen looked pained. She placed a set of manicured nails on her husband's arm. "Is that wise, dearest? Michael suffered that leg injury only last week."

"He's a royal vampire. The leg will be healed by now." The king smiled at us, wide enough to show most of his fangs. "You're welcome to any weapon in the armory."

Guards escorted us from the throne room to the armory. I watched with amusement as Alaric seemed to test every single weapon within reach.

"I'm impressed that he would show us his inner sanctum," Alaric commented. "If I were a different sort of vampire, I'd destroy his inventory before I left and then head straight back to New York from the battlefield."

The guard who'd escorted us cocked an eyebrow but said nothing.

"I hear we'll be facing death together," a voice boomed. A younger version of King Stefan swooped into the armory wearing a fine layer of silver armor and a mischievous grin.

"You must be Prince Michael," Alaric said.

Michael pumped Alaric's hand with enthusiasm. "So cool to meet you. I've heard so much about you. We have common friends, you know. Do you remember Mary-Kate Wellington? Devastatingly gorgeous. She spent a month at your place in Palm Beach."

I cut a glance at Alaric. "A whole month?"

The prince dragged an uncomfortable hand through his hair. "I have a big house with many bedrooms. Sometimes I have no idea who's staying there."

"Well, she enjoyed herself immensely, if that helps you at all." He turned to ponder the weapons on the wall. "I must warn you, I have my favorites."

"Is Mary-Kate one of them?" I quipped.

Michael tossed me a lazy smile. "I like you. You're the assassin, right? Very cool. I tried to persuade my parents to let me work as an assassin when I was younger, but Mother put her foot down."

Likely on his father's neck.

A blonde raced into the armory wearing a similar style of armor to Michael's, except hers was black.

"You're twins," I said, more to myself. They had the same shade of hair and matching sloped noses. Their eyes were a lovely cornflower blue.

"I'm the pretty one," Michael remarked, still eyeing his options.

I looked from one vampire to the other. "I thought it was good twin versus evil twin."

"That's only when he dares to wake me up before my alarm," Genevieve stated. "Then I'm all fangs."

"Genevieve, meet our esteemed guests," Michael said. "Prince Alaric and his assassin." His eyebrows inched together. "I'm sorry. I don't know your name."

"Britt."

"Charmed, I'm sure." Genevieve flashed a friendly smile as she sailed past us to admire the weapons on the wall. "I can't believe Father is letting us fight."

"I can't believe *Mother* is letting us." Michael selected a scythe and slashed it through the air. "I've always wanted to use one of these in a real battle."

I plucked the weapon from his hand. "If you don't mind me saying, I don't think it's your best bet, Your Highness."

"Why not?"

"We're confronting the Pey." I explained their background and the best weapons to use against them. "We'll try to negotiate with their leader first. That's Roma. If she takes responsibility and agrees to be tried for her crime, then we'll spare the rest of them." I cut a glance at Alaric. "Isn't that right, Your Highness?"

Alaric nodded. "Her confession might convince Mother and give us the time we need to intercept our troops."

Genevieve took a renewed interest in me. "You seem to know a lot about weapons and such. What's your story?"

"What about the word 'assassin' did you not understand?" Michael asked.

I exchanged amused looks with Alaric.

"This must be what it's like to have a sibling," Alaric mused.

"Oh, it's much worse," Genevieve said. "We're just

being polite in front of company." She chose a crossbow and held it up as though ready to test it.

"Good choice," I told her.

She gave her brother a smug look. "If only you were as smart as you are beautiful."

"We should really take Alexander with us," Michael said.

"Another brother?" I asked.

"Half brother, not that we're allowed to mention that part, especially in front of Mother." Michael pulled a throwing axe from the wall.

"Better," I said. "You'll want to keep as much distance between you and the Pey as possible."

"Why Alexander?" Alaric prompted.

"Because he's a skilled fighter and if he dies in the glory of battle, Mother would give thanks to the gods. She hates all of Father's bastards running around the compound like they belong here."

Genevieve didn't seem particularly bothered by the presence of half siblings.

"How many half siblings are there?" I asked.

"Depends," Michael said. "Are we only counting the ones Father acknowledges?"

Oh boy.

Genevieve opted for a set of throwing knives and strapped them to the utility belt around her hips for easy access. "I like Alexander, but I think his mother would object to him joining us. She'll think we plan to murder him on the battlefield and blame the Pey."

"His mother lives in the compound, too?" I asked.

"All Father's girlfriends do," Michael said. "How do you think they keep getting pregnant?"

King Stefan didn't seem all that irresistible to me. Then

again, I wasn't a vampire or a woman who desired a powerful mate. Alaric appealed to me in spite of those facts, not because of them.

"What material is your armor?" Alaric asked. "I've never seen anything like it."

Genevieve glanced down at her attire. "These were handmade by an in-house witch and her team. No poison arrows are making it through this baby."

"Let's hope they don't aim for your eye," Alaric said.

"It's Michael who's vulnerable," Genevieve pointed out. "The witches proposed black but Michael insisted on silver for his. They won't see me coming in this, but they'll spot the Silver Soldier over there a mile away." She angled her head toward her brother. "I tried to persuade him that black makes more sense than silver when you want the element of surprise, but Michael always has to be flashy in every sense of the word."

Michael shrugged. "What can I say? I like to make an entrance."

"The battlefield is not the place to make an entrance," I said. "Trust me."

"I don't know. I'm thinking Pomeranian horses pulling in my carriage."

"Do you mean Palladians?" I asked. "Pomeranians are a small dog breed."

Genevieve laughed. "I *love* the idea of you being dragged onto the battlefield by a crew of Pomeranians. Please make that happen."

"What about you, assassin?" Michael pressed. "You haven't chosen your weapons yet."

I walked the perimeter of the armory and studied the options. I needed to choose weapons I could use from a distance. On the adjacent wall, I spotted the updated version of the Monster Masher. Perfect.

"I wouldn't have pegged you for a gunslinger," Michael said.

I slid the Monster Masher into my holster. "This will get the job done."

Genevieve ran her fingers along the hilt of a sword that was still affixed to the wall. "I almost feel sorry for them."

"Have you fought in an actual battle before?" I asked as the four of us exited the armory.

"No, only training exercises," Michael said, "but we do them regularly. Father keeps us on a schedule."

"Which is one of the reasons this is so exciting," Genevieve interjected. "We get to break free of the dreaded schedule *and* we get to test our skills."

"How many vampires have you killed?" Michael asked as we made our way up the stairs to the main floor. "It's vampires that you target, right?"

"It used to be. I've worked security for House August for years now, though. They prefer that I not murder their civilian population."

"I've never seen anyone die," Michael interjected. "Is it horrible?"

"I don't derive pleasure from it."

"I guess that's one difference between vampires and witches," Michael said. "We're built to enjoy it the way advanced species like sex. Helps our species survive."

Genevieve nodded her approval. "You might want to jot that thought down on a napkin or something. That's the smartest thing I've ever heard you say."

# FOURTEEN

King Stefan's 'fastest fleet' included two magically-boosted, electric blue Hennessey Venoms. Michael's plea for a small plane had been promptly rejected by his mother. It seemed there'd been a dragon sighting in the airspace above Stevens Point and the queen refused to allow her children to travel by air.

"This is quite the upgrade from a minivan," I commented as I attempted to climb behind the U-shaped wheel.

Alaric placed a hand on my shoulder. "What do you think you're doing?"

I blinked. "Driving us to parley with the Pey."

"Do you think I'm going to give up the chance to get behind the wheel of one of these?" He shook his head. "No way."

"You're a prince. You can buy your own."

"And drive it where? Around Central Park? We don't have the open space for it in New York."

I opted not to argue. We had a more important issue to resolve.

From the sound of it, Michael and Genevieve were having the same argument. When I looked over from the passenger seat, Genevieve was behind the wheel. Good for her.

The car lived up to its reputation. I felt an adrenaline rush as Alaric ramped up our speed. I felt like we might break the sound barrier at any moment.

We located the Pey caravan in the same general vicinity as before. We parked far enough away that they wouldn't see us coming, although I assumed they had lookouts watching for approaching troops from either direction. They certainly wouldn't be expecting the four of us.

"Make that five of us," I said aloud. I pointed to the sky where a familiar silhouette was gliding toward us.

Alaric frowned. "George?"

The pygmy dragon landed on the roof of the Hennessey, prompting a gasp from Michael. "If you get so much as a scratch on that car, my father will mount your head over the fireplace."

Genevieve wriggled a friendly finger at the small dragon. "I wonder if you were the reason we weren't allowed to take the plane, you naughty boy."

"Follow the leader," I told George. "This is a parley, so no fire." We didn't have much time to convince Roma to turn herself in.

We made our way on foot to the edge of the caravan. The Pey seemed more terrifying now than they had during my scouting mission. While there were similarities with their vampire cousins, there was something primordial about them. The way they stood. The shape of their bodies. Their features. Their elongated fangs resembled those of a saber-toothed tiger.

I scanned the crowd and quickly identified their

leader. She wore a cape of feathers and her face was painted with streaks of white and red. Her dark hair was twisted into two coils on either side of her head. Her most dramatic feature was her eyes. Two bottomless pools of oil that threatened to drown me if I let them settle on me too long.

She was flanked on either side by taller, more muscular Pey. They held different weapons than the others, a scythe instead of a spear. I noticed a few others carrying quivers filled with what I assumed were poison-tipped arrows. The poison likely paralyzed the target long enough for the Pey to devour their flesh and blood.

"What's with the scythe?" Genevieve asked. "I can't decide if they're planning to fight or farm."

"See?" Michael said with a pointed look at me. "The scythe is a multi-purpose tool."

"How are there so many of them?" Genevieve wondered aloud.

"They've had years to assemble." They'd lived nomadic lives, swearing fealty to no House and picking up stray vampires along the way until their size swelled to the group here today.

"I don't get why they'd go to all this trouble just to eat," Michael remarked.

That was because the vampire didn't understand what it felt like to struggle. To belong nowhere and to no one. He couldn't grasp the desperation that drove the Pey.

But I could.

I understood the desire. If I'd encountered a witch version of the Pey when I was alone and struggling to survive, I probably would've joined them.

I inclined my head toward their fearless leader. "That's the one we want. Roma."

Alaric looked at the twins. "We go as a united front. Ready?"

Word started to spread among the Pey that there were visitors. I heard their hushed tones as Alaric strode toward their leader. Roma was in the middle of addressing one of her scythe-wielding companions.

"Roma," Alaric said in a commanding voice.

She turned to regard us. If she was surprised to see us, she hid it well. "It isn't often we receive visitors. What is your business with us?"

"I'm Prince Alaric of House August and these are my companions, Princess Genevieve and Prince Michael of House Nilsson, and my security advisor."

She lifted her chin a fraction. "Do you expect me to bow?"

I pointed to myself. "To me? Nah, I'm not big on formalities."

"We need to speak with you in private," Alaric said.

"I keep no secrets from my people," she declared. "Whatever you came to say, you may say it now for all to hear."

"Very well." Alaric cast a cautious glance around the ring of Pey. "We are here to charge you with the murder of my father, King Maxwell of House August, and ask that you surrender yourself into my custody."

"Don't forget multiple charges of incitement," I added. "It's a criminal offense to incite riots. Those werewolf packs only fought each other because you instigated them."

The leader of the Pey laughed. It was a horrible sound, the kind of screech that would startle you awake from a deep sleep. It picked at my bones and made me squirm.

"Prove it," she demanded.

"That's a job for the tribunal," Alaric said.

Roma sneered. "And what makes you think I'll come willingly?"

Alaric's fangs elongated. "Because if you agree to be taken into custody, then we won't massacre your people."

Her face turned to stone. "You dare threaten us?"

I moved closer to Alaric. "We know what your plan is and it won't work. The Houses aren't going to fight each other."

Her dark eyebrow spiked. "Really? Because my scouts tell me House August troops are en route to the House Nilsson border. Sounds like an impending battle to me."

"Too many lives will be lost if you don't turn yourself in," Alaric continued, "including those of your own kind." I was impressed that he was still pressing for diplomacy rather than resorting to violence. There was a leader buried in there yet.

Roma looked down her nose at him. "And what do you care of *my kind?*"

"Enough blood has been spilled," he insisted.

"I would think that would appeal to you, vampire." Her gaze turned to me. "And to you, Death Bringer."

Genevieve nudged me. "Cool. She knows who you are."

I kept my focus on Roma. "This isn't the way to get what you want."

She regarded me coolly. "Oh no? You have another suggestion? Perhaps we could bargain with House August for bodies. The problem is we don't like our meals cold, witch. Blood and flesh taste best when they're still warm."

"Listen, there's a place for all of us in this world. We don't need to incite a war to find it."

Roma laughed again and I fought the urge to cover my ears. "And where is your place, slave of House August? You may as well have come here with a collar and a leash held by your master." She gestured to the prince.

Genevieve's hands cemented to her narrow hips. "And what about me?"

Roma sneered. "A child with no discernible talent who will bring her House to ruin."

Michael grasped his sister's arms to prevent her from unsheathing her knife.

"You're not looking at the big picture," Alaric said. "You'll do your Angels of Mercy act for one battle and then you'll have a target on your back. Our Houses will hunt you to extinction as payback."

Roma sneered. "You idiot. This isn't a play for fast food. My goal is to remove the two most powerful Houses to pave the path for humans. To restore them to their rightful place on this earth."

"That's awfully magnanimous of you," Michael said, "but it won't happen without sunlight."

"They're not being altruistic," I said, keeping my gaze pinned on Roma. "They want the return of war. Humans on the battlefield were their main food source. They've been suffering ever since the start of the Eternal Night."

"My people are dying. Our numbers have dwindled to only this." She waved a hand toward her followers. "Desperate times call for desperate measures."

Alaric held out a hand. "Turn yourself in, Roma. Save your people from slaughter."

"I'd sooner die," Roma snarled. She whipped a hand into the air. "Attack!"

Genevieve was the first to react. The princess unleashed a knife in each hand and *threw*. The blades sailed through the air and struck Roma in the right shoulder and left torso. The Pey queen simply pinched the handles between two fingers and dropped each knife to the ground.

I shuffled backward. We needed to retreat and wait for House Nilsson forces to arrive. We couldn't take on all these Pey without help. Even given my newfound ability, my magic could likely only hold so many of them at once.

The Pey tightened their circle around us.

"Is anyone else getting a monkey-in-the-middle vibe?" Michael asked.

Genevieve thrust back her shoulders, her head held high. "You might as well let us go. You won't gain anything from hurting us."

"On the contrary," Roma said, and sniffed the air. "At least one of you smells delicious."

"Cannibal," Michael spat.

Fangs out, Genevieve charged. The vampire leaped into the air and collided with Roma. They tumbled to the ground.

An arrow whizzed past me, skimming my shoulder. The Pey were on the offensive. Not the response I was hoping for.

As I whipped out the Monster Masher, the tip of a spear crashed into the gun and sent it sailing. I ducked the spear as it swung back toward me.

My heart thumped like a wild bird in a cage. I wrapped my fingers around the pointy end of the spear and yanked. My attacker went flying. I kept moving forward and used the spear against the onslaught of Pey. I pushed the spear through the flesh of the Pey in front of me and relieved him of his own. I spun a spear in each hand and wielded them like escrima sticks. I tried to use magic, but I couldn't focus on one attacker long enough to form a connection.

Nobody prepares you for the chaos of a battlefield.

To their credit, Genevieve and Michael didn't fight like spoiled royals. They were strong and brave and seemed to revel in the heat of battle. Vampires had become so elegant and refined over the years that the population seemed to collectively forget that vampires were once baser creatures. Their thirst for blood overrode all their other senses. The vampires of old would never have fought side-by-side with a witch. Roma and the Pey seemed to have more in common with the pre-Eternal Night vampires than the vampires of House August or Nilsson.

A massive Pey ran straight for me and used his chest as a battering ram. I sailed backward, losing a spear in the process. I drove the remaining spear into the ground and dragged it across the ground to slow my landing.

As the battle raged on, I lost sight of my companions. I spotted Roma in the middle of it all, her curved fangs gleaming in the dim light. She was barking commands at her minions that I couldn't hear.

"Britt, over here!"

I glanced over to see Genevieve waving to me. It only took a second to understand why. The remaining Pey were lined up in a row to let their poison-tipped arrows fly. They were forming a firing squad.

I hustled backward, continuing to face the enemy as I put distance between us. Turning my back on flying arrows seemed like a very bad idea.

George hovered above me, acting as my bodyguard. Any time an arrow came close, the pygmy dragon blew a stream of fire and disintegrated it. Sometimes I wondered what a team of dragons could achieve. It was often said that whichever species learned to control dragons could take over the world. So far the dragons resisted the call of a master. They were wild and did as they pleased, but I often thought it was only a matter of time before someone managed to domesticate them.

Then again, if magic users ever got their act together and worked as one, they, too, had the ability to remove vampires from the top of the food chain. But now wasn't the time to contemplate a future without vampires. Without vampires in my corner, right now I'd be dead.

"Where's Michael?" Genevieve's voice rang out and I heard the note of alarm.

"I see him!" I pointed across the field to a silhouette running toward us.

Genevieve sagged with relief.

Halfway to us, an arrow skimmed his shoulder and I heard a sharp intake of breath beside me. Michael stumbled and Genevieve tried to rush forward, but Alaric held her back.

"You're dead if you go back out there," the prince said.

Michael continued to run as another arrow skimmed a calf.

Genevieve jerked toward me. "You're a witch. Can't you do something?"

"I don't have that kind of magic," I told her.

Genevieve pushed against Alaric's arm, but he maintained a firm grip on her.

Michael carried on, dodging arrows in an impressive display of acrobatics. The ones that managed to hit him bounced off his magical armor. The king had trained him well.

George helped us out by blowing fire behind Michael to create a fiery wall between us and our attackers.

Michael finally reached us and his sister threw her arms around him. "You're such an idiot."

There seemed to be an infinite supply of arrows. Their

offensive measures were more in line with an army than Angels of Mercy that swept the battlefield after the violence was over.

The fire diminished, leaving us exposed. If I acted swiftly, I could create a ward that would give us enough time to escape.

Once the flow of arrows slowed, I made my move. "I'll meet you at the cars! Go!"

They ran toward the cars and I ran in the opposite direction. All I had to do was leave drops of my blood across the ground where the wall of fire had just stood. Block the arrows and buy us time to get away. It seemed like a simple plan—until I reached for my dagger to draw blood and found them gone.

Shit.

I looked up in time to see dozens of poison-tipped arrows whizzing toward me. I didn't have a suit of magical armor. If a single point made contact with me, it was game over. I needed to access my blood. Naturally this was the one time I wasn't bleeding in the middle of a fight. My vampire compatriots were too far away for their fangs to be useful.

Great gods above.

I bit my hand hard but didn't manage to break the skin.

There was no time.

Above me I felt the air stir and tipped my head toward the sky. "George, go! Fly away!" There was no need for both of us to die.

The dragon lowered his body in front of mine and spread his wings wide.

"George, no!"

Even if a blast of fire disintegrated most of the arrows, it would only take one to fell the pygmy dragon.

Heat radiated from his small body as he faced the enemy.

He didn't simply breathe fire.

He became it.

Flames engulfed his body and lit up his wings. The dragon shone like a burning star in the night sky. Instinctively I closed my eyes and threw up my hands to block the extreme light. Heat blasted through me, warming my skin.

What was he doing? I'd seen the dragon spew fire more times than I could count, but this was the first time I'd witnessed him self-immolate.

"George, stop," I begged. "You're burning up." If the dragon continued, he would collapse like a dying star. I couldn't let him sacrifice himself for me or anyone else. If one of us deserved to live, it was sweet George.

The intensity of the heat forced me backward and I ended up curled on the ground in a ball with my hands over my head. A moment later a larger body curved over mine. The scent of grapefruit and frankincense filled my nostrils.

"It'll be okay, Britt," Alaric said in a soothing voice. "Just stay down."

"You were supposed to go back to the car with the others."

"Since when do I take orders from you?" he murmured in my ear.

I felt every inch of the vampire's body pressing against mine as the fire raged. It was both heaven and hell encapsulated in a single moment. Once the heat and light dissipated, Alaric slid off me. I lifted my head in time to see a trail of black ash drifting to the ground.

George was gone.

Hot tears stung my eyes and spilled down my cheeks. A primal sound erupted and I realized it was coming from me.

The guttural noise ripped from my throat and I clawed at the air as though I could somehow reclaim him from space and time.

Still on my knees, my gaze moved from the pile of black ash steaming on the ground to the scene beyond.

The sound of twin engines erupted and two cars sped toward us, pushing past caravans and mowing down everything in their path. They divided around me and headed straight for the remaining Pey.

Whatever George had done, he'd taken half the Pey with him. They were sprawled across the ground coated in a fine layer of black ash.

The cars plowed through enemy lines and skidded around for a return trip.

Alaric helped me to my feet and we went in search of Roma. We found the Pey leader on the ground amidst her fallen soldiers. Her dark eyes were just blinking open. I didn't wait for her to fully regain consciousness. My magic snapped to attention and I crouched beside her to let it loose in Roma's blood.

I turned to see Michael and Genevieve looming over us.

"We'll take her to the Hennessey before the others recover," Genevieve said. "Under the circumstances, I don't think Father will mind if you drive it back to New York."

I wouldn't be able to maintain the amount of focus needed to control her all the way back to New York, but I could slow the blood flow enough to keep her in a catatonic state until she was safely in custody.

I held up my wrist that still sported the portal bracelet. "You and Michael drive the cars home. I have a better idea."

But first I had to say goodbye to my best friend.

Struggling to maintain my composure, I crossed the field

to find the dragon's remains. "Oh, George," I whispered. "Why did you do this?"

Despite my best efforts, tears slipped past my eyelashes and splashed on the pile of ash. Ringlets of smoke curled from the ashes and I took a step backward. A flicker of movement snagged my gaze and I watched as the ash began to shift like sand in the wind.

"What's happening?" Alaric asked.

I didn't even realize the vampire was beside me. "I have no idea."

The deep black of the ashes began to lighten and rubescent streaks formed, followed by burnt orange and auburn. The embers seemed to be reigniting.

"Is it just my imagination or are those ashes moving?" I asked.

"Must be the breeze," Genevieve said from over my shoulder.

"What breeze?" Michael licked his finger and held it up. "There's no wind."

Lumps formed and gathered into a single, connected shape.

Michael pointed. "Wait, are those…wings?"

They were, in fact, wings. My spirits rose as the creature's head did the same, followed by his body.

My voice cracked as his name passed my lips. "George."

The dragon's eyes opened and landed on me. His mouth opened, emitting a tiny squeak.

"I can't believe it. You're alive, you incredible dragon." I lunged for my small companion.

"Assassin, I've got news for you," Michael said. "Your friend isn't a pygmy dragon."

I engulfed him in a hug and kissed his bumpy head.

"What are you talking about? Wings. Fire. What else could he be?"

Michael motioned to the remaining ashes. "He's a phoenix."

I stared at the Not Pygmy Dragon. "Wait. You're not a dragon?"

George burped, pushing a small puff of smoke toward my face. I fanned it away.

Alaric scrutinized our recently risen companion. "Why doesn't he have feathers?"

"Despite popular belief, a phoenix isn't actually a bird," Michael explained. "They're just related. I'd be willing to bet the species is a closer relative of dragons."

"Michael's a science nerd in case you haven't noticed," Genevieve said.

"I don't care what he is." George was my friend and that was all that mattered. I wagged a finger at him. "Don't you ever self-immolate again, do you hear me?"

The phoenix hung his head.

I looked at Alaric. "Is there a 'no phoenix' policy in New York that I need to be aware of?"

"Even if there was, my first order of business at home would be to reverse it." The prince bent down to pat the top of George's head. "How would you feel about being knighted, little friend?"

George rubbed the side of his head against Alaric's arm.

"Sir George it is," the prince announced.

## FIFTEEN

In the safety of the New York compound, Roma offered a full confession and the House August army was summoned home. Queen Dionne was repentant for her stubborn refusal to listen to her son. According to Olis, she sent a gift basket brimming with specialty blood and House wines to House Nilsson, along with a note of apology.

I spent my recovery time making good on promises. It wasn't hard to locate David Boreas. Alaric instructed Olis to give me the information, which arrived via carrier pigeon early this morning. Too early, I might add, but that was a conversation to be had with Olis later.

Once the phone line was working, I called Meghan to deliver the news. "I have the address, but I'm going on record that I'd rather you not pursue it."

"Because you don't want to be responsible for David's death?"

"Because I don't want to be responsible for yours." Despite our uncomfortable beginning, I'd quickly grown fond of the werewolf. "I know you have every reason to despise me and I don't blame you for it, but I like you,

Meghan. I'm about to start fresh in this world—a clean slate—and I could really use all the friends I can get."

There was silence on the other end of the line. Finally she said, "I'll take it under advisement."

The call ended. I stared at the phone and hoped that Meghan found the strength to break the cycle of violence. She deserved peace.

A knock on the window startled me. I hurried across the room and laughed when I saw Alaric perched on the ledge.

"Did you flutter and transform at an awkward moment?"

"No. I climbed up the fire escape like old times." He thrust a hand forward. The smell hit me before I realized what he held in his hand.

My stomach gurgled. "Are you for real?" I snatched the taco from his hand and inhaled the smell of guacamole. "How?"

He climbed through the window. "I have my methods."

I bit into the taco and nearly melted into a puddle on the floor.

"I wanted to bring you something special as a thank you."

"You don't have to thank me," I said through bites of heavenly taco. "I was holding up my end of the bargain."

"You went above and beyond and you know it."

"Your mother freed me, so I got what I wanted."

He cocked his head. "Did you?"

Swallowing the last bite of taco, I met his gaze. "I'm a free witch. You're alive and well. I got a taco. So yes. All the boxes have been ticked."

Inwardly I was less confident. Now that I was no longer a part of House August, I had no reason to see him again.

No reason to stay in New York, in fact. I could go anywhere. Reinvent myself.

Alaric seemed to sense my thought process. "Are you leaving town? You don't have to give up the apartment. That's part of the package. I made sure of it."

"I haven't decided what I'm doing yet." I was comfortable here. For better or worse, New York was home to me. "Anyway, you'll be busy helping your mother run an empire."

"Not helping. Running. My mother has decided to turn her crown over to me. She'll become queen regent."

The news didn't surprise me. Queen Dionne made no bones about the fact that she wasn't meant to lead. Her breakdown after King Maxwell's death must've solidified her decision.

I studied his stoic face. "Are you okay with that?"

"I'm getting there."

"You're nothing like him, you know. And you can be a different kind of leader and still be effective, one that shows compassion and grace to all species."

His lips formed a half smile. "Since when do you associate me with compassion?"

I smiled back. "It's a recent discovery."

"I'm going to make mistakes."

"Nobody's perfect." I whistled softly. "Wow. King Alaric."

He reached for my hand. "That title comes with certain perks."

"Free booze?"

His fingers skimmed the soft flesh between my thumb and index finger, igniting sparks deep in my core.

"I was thinking more along the lines of a date to my coronation." He continued to caress my skin. "Are you interested? It won't be like the vineyard. This time will be different, I swear it."

I looked into his green eyes and let my imagination drift.

He leaned down and I instinctively tilted my head to allow him access. His lips traveled down my neck to my collarbone and I felt the prick of his fangs. Shivers racked my body.

"Say yes, Britt," he murmured.

I longed to say yes. To have what I'd once wanted most in the world.

But that time had passed.

"No." I grabbed the back of his hair and tugged his head to an upright position. "I can't. Find yourself a lovely vampire to witness your ascension. Marry her. Have lots of royal vampire babies." The words stung as they passed my lips.

"In other words, be like King Stefan? No thank you. I've glimpsed that life up close and it isn't for me." In one swift motion, he turned me around and pinned me to the wall. "I'm only interested in one lovely woman and she's right here. My knight in shining leather pants."

He pressed against me and I nearly succumbed. As much as I'd tried to squelch it, the heat between us was as vibrant as ever. One touch and I'd come undone.

Flames shot past us and singed the wall. Alaric tore himself off me and whipped around to confront the attacker.

"What the hell, George?" the vampire demanded.

My heartbeat slowed to a normal rate and I returned to my senses. "Thank you for the taco, Your Highness. Please let me know when the coronation will be."

"You'll at least attend?"

"No, I want to make sure to be out of town that day. The crowds will be a nightmare."

He didn't react. "Enjoy your freedom, Britt. I expect great things from you."

"I find it best not to have expectations. That way I can't be disappointed."

"See you around, George."

The phoenix burped a puff of grey smoke.

Alaric returned to the window, transformed into a green and gold butterfly, and flew away.

I ran to the window and closed it. My knees nearly buckled as I pulled myself together.

"Thank you, George. You did the right thing."

The phoenix made a happy, high-pitched noise and flew back to the bedroom.

I decided to focus on a menial task. Anything to keep me from thinking about the mistake I may or may not have just made. I looked at the dirty dishes that I'd left in the sink before my adventure began. That would do.

I turned on the faucet and prepared for a deep dive. Just because I didn't cook didn't mean my kitchen was clean.

A knock at the door interrupted my sudsy meditation. I pictured Alaric in the corridor with a whole tray of tacos spelling out the words 'say yes.' It was a silly sentiment and I quickly dismissed it. No more fantasies.

"Come in," I yelled, ready to chastise the prince for coming back so quickly.

A wizard entered the apartment.

"Olis, what are you doing here?"

He swiveled toward me. "You seem surprised to see me."

"You're too late, boss. No more assignments for this

witch. The queen held up her end of the bargain. I'm a free woman now."

Olis didn't smile. "Congratulations. It isn't the reason I'm here."

"Oh? Came to bid me a fond farewell? I wouldn't object to a parting gift. I accept money, baked goods, a bottle of wine..."

He clasped his hands in front of him. "Do you remember your mishap with the magical bomb and the bus?"

"I think you're forgetting a salient detail. It was the *Big Apple* tour bus. I know how much you love that nickname. Wouldn't want you to forget."

Olis closed his eyes briefly, likely praying for strength to get through this conversation. "What do you know about the Trinity Group?"

"Never heard of them. Why?"

He motioned for me to come closer. "Join me for a drink. There is very little time and much to discuss."

"Can't leave. Liam is back from the Wasteland and I'm meeting him for an update. He gets impatient if I'm late. Trust me, you don't want Liam impatient. He might detonate something."

"Fine. We'll discuss it here." His gaze swept the apartment as though we might be overheard.

"You seem on edge, Olis. Relax. House August is intact. Your job is secure."

"Only because you did yours."

Something in his tone struck a chord in me. I grabbed a hand towel and dried the plate in my hand. "You recommended me to the queen for that assignment. Why?"

"Because you're the best at what you do."

I examined him closely. "The odds weren't in our favor. How did you know I'd succeed?"

"Truthfully I didn't."

"But you wanted to see."

His eye twitched. It was a small movement, but it told me what I needed to know.

A thought occurred to me. "Was tracking the mint part of your test?"

"Not so much tracking the mint itself as seeing what you did once you found the wizards responsible."

I stared at him agape. Olis had been playing me and I'd been too blind to see it.

"Why me?" When he didn't answer, I set down the plate and gave him my hardest stare. "Let me try this again. Why? Me?"

The wizard seemed to resolve an internal argument. "Because I believe you are part of a prophecy."

Laughing, I picked up a soapy glass. "You can't be serious."

"Am I ever anything else?"

I looked at him. No. Never. "What's the prophecy about?"

"The return of sunlight to this world."

My eyebrows lifted. "That's a major prophecy."

"It is."

I rinsed the glass. "What does that have to do with the magical bomb?"

"Those wizards you met are nothing but a diversion. Their entire role is to keep security preoccupied so that more important activities can continue undetected."

"You ordered me to track the mint. You knew the trail would lead to them."

"And I knew you would let them go—at least, I

suspected you would. The fact that you proved me right was a point in your favor."

I turned off the faucet. "How do I fit in to this prophecy?"

"You are one of three elements necessary to succeed."

I scoffed. "I'm not an element. I'm a living, breathing witch."

"A living, breathing witch with a certain rare ability. We believe we know the identity of another, which leaves only one to find."

I set down the glass and stared at him. "And how am I supposed to bring back the sun? Find the staff of Ra and unlock a secret portal?"

"That part we have yet to determine, only that you have an important role to play."

"And you're sure of this? All because I successfully returned the prince to New York?"

"A lesser being couldn't have managed it. Your success proves you are the one we've been searching for."

I squinted at the wizard. "So you were willing to sacrifice me just to see if I was the right 'element?'" I used air quotes around 'element.'

"We'd like you to join our cause, Britt. There are people you should meet."

"You're a traitor to House August."

He blinked in surprise. "I know you and the prince have a strange attachment to each other, but you can't possibly want to live under vampire rule forever. You're free now. You have no obligation to the House."

"It's treason either way." The Director of Security for House August was a traitor. Unreal.

"I ask again—will you join us?"

My jaw unhinged. "No, I won't join you. How many

other innocent witches have you thrown away like garbage because she didn't fit the mold? I've got news for you. I'm not disposable."

I threw the towel at him. It landed on his head. He swiped it away and placed it neatly on the arm of the sofa.

"You're choosing vampires over your own kind?"

"My own kind?" My voice sounded bitter and hollow even to my own ears. "In case you missed it, my own kind haven't exactly treated me well. How do you think I ended up here in the first place?"

"You risked your life for the children in the Wasteland..."

"That was different." I emerged from the kitchen and crossed the room to join him at the door.

He peered at me, curious. "How?"

"They were young. Innocent."

"Don't hold your past against the rest of us, Britt. We need you. Our survival depends on it. Don't choose the enemy."

"I'm not choosing them. I'm choosing me." I yanked open the door. "Thanks for dropping by, Olis."

His gaze intensified. "You realize your refusal puts you in danger."

"I didn't ask to know too much. That's on you."

He shook his head. "It won't matter to them."

"Tell your zealot friends I won't rat you out to the prince. I'm not interested in getting involved." I wasn't about to jeopardize my freedom over a ridiculous prophecy.

"It won't matter what you say. You're a security risk now."

"So I'm either with you or against you?" I blew out a breath. "Thanks for dropping this flaming bag of dog shit on my doorstep. Very generous of you after all I've been through."

Olis rested a hand gently on my shoulder. "Take care, Britt. You have a target on your back now. I won't be the one to do it, but someone else won't hesitate."

"Good thing targets are my specialty." I practically kicked him out the door.

I turned around to see George hovering in the doorway. "Don't look at me like that. I refuse to be a pawn in their game."

I marched back to the kitchen to finish the task I'd started. I scrubbed angrily, taking out my aggression on the dirty dishes.

"Let them come," I told the phoenix as defiance simmered under my skin. "I've survived worse."

I was Britt, the Blood Witch. Free of shackles. Free to live my life on my own terms. I certainly wasn't about to trade one collar for another.

I was nobody's witch.

YOU DON'T WANT to miss the continuation of Britt's story in **Red Rook**, book 2 in the *Midnight Empire: The Restoration* series. For more information on my books or to sign up for my newsletter, please visit my website at www.annabelchase.com.

Printed in Great Britain
by Amazon